THE BOY Lolli POWELL NEXTDOOR

This book is a work of fiction. Any resemblance to persons, places, or events is purely coincidental.

***

Cover from: Bill Wilkinson at format-your-book-4u.com.

DEDICATION

This book is dedicated to Earl. Thank you for giving my life a happily-ever-after ending. I don't tell you as often as I should how much I love you and appreciate you.

ACKNOWLEDGMENTS

A special thanks to my beta-readers. Thank you for your time and input. It helped tremendously.

.

ALSO BY THE AUTHOR

As Lolli Powell:

The Wrong Kind of Man (romantic suspense)

The Body on the Barstool (cozy mystery)

As Laurel Heidtman:

Whiteout (thriller)

Eden series (mystery)*:*
Catch A Falling Star
Bad Girls
A Convenient Death (coming early 2017)

Chapter 1

A car Laney Mitchell had never seen before sat in the driveway of the unoccupied house next door. It was a late model white Ford Focus with Ohio tags, and it definitely wasn't the car Jack, the guy who mowed the Davidsons' yard, drove. Jack had mentioned that Linda Hall, the Davidsons' daughter, had told him they'd soon be putting the house on the market. Maybe the car belonged to a real estate agent or even Linda herself. It had been years since she'd seen Linda. Would she even recognize the woman?

Should she call the police? After all, there hadn't been any visitors to the house—other than Jack every week or so to mow and check up on things—in the five years since Linda had moved her mother and father to California so she could watch over them in their old age. It was nearly nine o'clock in the evening—a little late for a real estate agent to be stopping by. The house was still furnished. There might not be much to steal, but still. . . .

She shook her head. She was being ridiculous. Burglars didn't park their getaway cars in the driveway of the house they were burgling. It was probably a real estate agent or even Linda herself. Better to just knock on the door and find out.

Standing up straight and squaring her shoulders, Laney strode up the walk to the Davidsons' door, vacillating between feeling like a paranoid busybody neighbor and a fool for walking into a potentially dangerous situation. The smart thing to do would be to go into her own house and keep an eye out the window. If she saw someone carrying the TV to the car, she could call the police then.

But she'd seldom done the smart thing. Getting pregnant in college and marrying Greg was evidence of that. She raised her hand and knocked on the door.

A light came on in the living room, its glow oozing from between the closed draperies covering the bay window, and Laney relaxed. A burglar wouldn't turn on the light when someone knocked at the door. A second later, she heard the deadbolt disengage and the door opened.

She had expected a real estate agent in a suit or a nice dress, or maybe Linda herself. She hadn't expected a half-naked young man with wet hair.

Tall and tan, the man was dressed only in a pair of worn jeans and a towel slung over his right shoulder. No shirt, no shoes or socks, and the jeans were unsnapped and only half-zipped. His chest was broad and muscled, his abdomen flat and hard. Curly dark brown hair, thicker across his pectorals and thinning as it moved lower, led her eyes downward to the half-open fly of his jeans. He didn't appear to be wearing any underwear. His chiseled cheekbones, strong jaw, and perfect nose were framed by damp wavy brown hair that hung slightly below his ears. His hazel eyes were warm and friendly as he smiled at her.

"Hey," he said. "What can I do for you?"

Before she could stop herself, images flashed through Laney's mind as she thought of what this gorgeous creature could do for her. She was appalled at her reaction. Good Lord, she thought, I'm nearly old enough to be this man's mother!

"I'm sorry to bother you," she said, pushing the thoughts from her mind. "I live next door and I don't usually see anyone around this house. I thought I'd better check and make sure everything is okay."

"Bryce Adams," he said, extending his right hand. "This is my grandparents' house. My mother is putting it on the market, and I'm here to fix whatever needs fixing."

"Bryce Adams?" Laney's eyes widened. "I used to babysit you!"

He leaned closer, squinting to get a better look at her in the light spilling from the living room. "Laney Harris?"

"It's Laney Mitchell now." She extended her hand. "It's nice to see you again after all these years."

"Laney Mitchell?" He looked surprised, but took her hand and shook. Letting it go, he stood to the side and motioned for her to enter. "Come in. Please."

"Oh, no," she said. "I didn't mean to bother you. Now that I know you belong here, I need to get home."

"Aw, come on, have some tea with me. I just got out of the shower and was going to fix some anyway. I like herbal tea before hitting the sack—helps relax me. We can catch up on the past—wow, how long has it been—fifteen, twenty years?"

She hesitated for a moment before stepping into the house. Truth was, she was too keyed up to sleep after dealing with Greg all day. Maybe herbal tea and the distraction of conversation with a man who didn't want anything from her might be just the thing to help her unwind.

As he led her through the living room to the kitchen, her memory rewound twenty-six years—for that's how long it had been since she'd spent time with Bryce Adams. Only he had been "little Brycie" back then. A precocious and adorable child with big innocent eyes who loved nothing more than to cuddle up on her lap while she read to him. Laney had been fifteen with a thriving babysitting business, but Brycie had been her favorite.

"I'm surprised you remember me," she said. "You were only five the last time I saw you."

"A man never forgets his first love." He grinned. "I don't know if you knew it back then, but I had the biggest crush on you."

Laney laughed. "You did?"

"Oh, yeah. Told my mom I was going to marry you when I was all grown up." He opened a cabinet and removed two white ceramic mugs. "I hope water heated in the microwave and teabags are okay."

"That's fine."

"So," he said, as he filled the mugs with water from the kitchen tap. "Since your last name is Mitchell now, I guess you didn't wait for me to walk you down the aisle?"

"No. Sorry. If I had only known, I would have waited," she joked. "How about you? Are you married?"

"Nope. Guess I never met anyone who could hold a candle to you," he joked back.

He put the cups in the microwave, set the time and pressed the Start button, then turned to face her, leaning against the kitchen counter.

"Kids?" he asked.

"One. A daughter, Deanna. Dee. She's a sophomore at Ohio State—oops, I mean a junior. Or will be in the fall. Dee and some friends are driving around the country for a few weeks before heading home, which is why I keep forgetting school is out for the summer."

"You don't look like a woman with a college-age daughter." His eyes moved slowly down over her body, then back up to her face. "You look as good as I remember."

Laney flushed. "That's kind of you to say."

"Not being kind, just telling the truth. You obviously take good care of yourself. You work out?"

She nodded. "My ex and I own three fitness clubs in the area. Bodies for Life. I work out at one or the other a few times a week and do a little jogging when the weather is good."

"Your ex? You're not married now?"

"Greg and I have been divorced for three years."

"So I have a chance after all?"

She laughed. "You are so funny."

The timer beeped and the microwave shut off. Bryce set the cups on the counter, dropped a bag of chamomile tea into each of them and crossed to the breakfast bar separating the kitchen from the dining nook in the corner of the living room.

"Have a seat." He set cups on the counter and pulled out a stool for her, taking the one at the end for himself.

"So what do you do?" she asked, carefully sipping the hot tea.

"Oh, this and that," he said. "I'm a licensed massage therapist, for one thing."

"Really?" she said. "We thought about making massage available at Bodies, but we don't really have the space for a private room. I wish we had thought of it when we built the clubs."

"You're divorced, but you're still a co-owner with your ex?"

She nodded. "Part of the divorce agreement. Neither of us could afford to buy the other out and neither of us was going to just give up our share, so we worked it out. I'm a CPA. I took care of that side of the business when Greg and I were married, and I still do."

"Must get awkward at times."

"You can say *that* again." She felt herself start to tense. "Sometimes I think I'd have been better off just letting him take the clubs."

He shook his head. "You did the right thing. Nobody should have to give up something that is rightfully theirs."

"So how are your grandparents?" Time for a change of subject or she'd never relax enough to get to sleep, chamomile or no chamomile. "And your mom."

"Granddad just passed three weeks ago," Bryce said, his expression turning sad. "Lung cancer. A month shy of his eightieth birthday."

"Oh, I'm so sorry," Laney said. "I remember him as a nice man."

"He was the best. Grandma's health is good, although his death took the wind out of her sails. She lives with Mom and my stepdad."

"Doris told me Linda had remarried." Laney thought for a moment. "Doris and Ed moved to California, what—three years ago? It seems like she told me Linda had remarried quite a while before that."

"Mom and Ben have been married about ten years," he said. "Mom waited until I was out of the house before she'd even date. Said one man at a time was enough for her to take care of."

They both laughed.

"I remember now," Laney said. "Your mom was always funny. I had forgotten that."

They drank their tea in silence for a few moments. Laney found herself remembering things she hadn't thought of in years. Bryce's father had died in a car accident when Bryce was less than a year old. Ed and Doris Davidson had moved their daughter and grandson in with them, caring for them while Linda went to nursing school. Linda had had a V.A. scholarship her last year of school so she owed the V.A. a year of nursing. Bryce's paternal grandparents lived in San Diego and, when Linda graduated, they convinced her to fulfill her commitment at the V.A hospital there. Doris and Ed had been sad to see their daughter and grandson go, but they understood that she wanted to get away from the town that held so many sad memories for her.

Laney had started babysitting for Bryce when she was fifteen and he was four. It was only an occasional thing, since Doris usually watched Bryce while her daughter took classes or did her clinicals. Whenever Doris and Ed had things to do on a weekend or wanted a night out, though, they called on the teenager next door. He was five when Linda graduated and they moved to southern California.

"Is Linda still a nurse?"

"A nurse practitioner midwife," Bryce said. "She went back to school when I started junior high."

"That's impressive."

"My mom's a smart woman," Bryce said, his pride evident.

"How long are you here for?" she asked.

"Not sure," he said. "I've got a few things to take care of, including sprucing up the house—interior paint, new carpet, that sort of thing. It needs a little updating to increase the chances of it selling at the asking price."

"You're probably anxious to get back to California."

"Well, now that I've reconnected with the love of my life, California can wait."

He smiled, but it was the kind of smile a man gives a woman when he's imagining what he might do to her in bed, not the kind of smile a man gives a woman when he's joking. Laney felt herself grow warm in places she had no business growing warm. She had been his babysitter!

"I can see you got your mother's sense of humor," she said, making a conscious decision to ignore the look and take the comment as a joke. Chances were good she was imagining the intent of that look anyway. She swallowed the remainder of her tea and stood.

"I need to get home and get some sleep," she said. "It's been a long day. Thank you for the tea and the conversation."

"I'd like to see your clubs," Bryce said. "Is it a problem to get a guest pass or two so I can work out while I'm here?"

"No problem at all," Laney said. "I don't have any with me, but if you have time tomorrow, stop by Bodies in the Rosedale Mall out by the interstate. I'll be there all day. Do you know where the mall is?"

"Actually I do," he said. "I stopped there on my way in to pick up some toiletries and some extra underwear and socks."

Even though you don't wear them, Laney thought before she could stop herself. She turned and started toward the front door, hoping he hadn't noticed her eyes drift downward to the front of his jeans. She also hoped he hadn't noticed her disappointment when she saw that he had zipped the rest of the way up when she wasn't looking.

"Tell you what," he said. "How about I come by in the morning, work out for a while, then take you to lunch? I assume the clubs have showers so I can clean up first."

"They do have showers, but it isn't necessary to take me to lunch."

"I didn't mean it as a thank you for the guest passes," he said. "I'd just like to have lunch with you. And I promise you won't have to make up a game to get me to eat all my vegetables."

Laney burst out laughing. It had always been a chore to get little Brycie to eat his veggies. She had had to be inventive and turn it into a game or a contest to get even half down him.

"You remember that?"

"I told you—a man never forgets anything about his first love."

"Oh, boy!" She shook her head, still laughing. "You are really something!"

She turned at the door and extended her hand.

"Thanks again for the tea, Bryce. And for the conversation. It was fun."

"A handshake? A guy only gets a handshake from his first love after all this time?" His mouth twisted up on one end in the cutest little grin Laney thought she'd ever seen. "I think a hug would be more appropriate."

Before she could react, he stepped forward, wrapped his arms around her and drew her into his naked chest. He pressed her against his body, his palms splayed across her back moving in slow circular motions. For a second she didn't move, then her own arms wrapped themselves around his body almost, it seemed, of their own volition. Her face was turned to the right and her left cheek rested against his muscular shoulder, his still damp hair tickling her forehead. He smelled of soap—Irish Spring, if she wasn't mistaken—and shampoo. She breathed deeply of it.

"It was great finding you again," he mumbled into her neck.

She felt his right hand move to her collar. He pulled it back and planted a quick kiss on the spot where her neck joined her shoulder, causing her to shiver involuntarily.

"Wead me a story, Waney," he said in a little boy voice.

She pulled away, laughing, and smacked him on the shoulder.

"Stop it! I cannot believe you remember doing that!" She shook her head. "I didn't until just now. I'd read you a story, but you never got enough—you'd always kiss my neck and ask for another. You loved being read to."

"Yeah, I did," he said. "But what I loved even more was cuddling with you."

"You were a sweet little boy," she said. She turned away and hurried out the door to the safety zone of the front porch. Without turning, she waved a goodbye. "See you in the morning."

***

Laney shut her front door, locked it, then collapsed against it, her heart racing. Wow, she thought. That cute little boy I used to babysit has sure grown up! Her neck still tingled where he had kissed her. She knew the hug and the kiss had just been playful and friendly. He was the kind of guy who would automatically turn on the charm with any female he met, whether she was five or ninety-five. She'd known men like that before, but this was the first time one had caused her to have what her grandmother would have called "impure thoughts." If she didn't get a grip, she was going to have to take a cold shower before going to bed.

One plus of exposure to Bryce Adams was that it had driven all thoughts of Greg from her mind, even if it was only temporary. Her ex was starting to be a major pain in the butt. Well, no, he'd been that for a while, but now he was escalating. He had somehow gotten it into his head that they still had a chance together, but that ship had sailed.

She had met Greg during her freshman year of college. He was a senior, good-looking, and on the football team—naturally it had been an ego booster when he noticed her. She had worried that when he graduated he would move on to someone else, but they stayed together. Halfway through her sophomore year, she became pregnant. Greg was thrilled, her parents not so much.

Greg had taken a job as a salesman with a sports equipment company right after graduation. The pay was good, he could support a family, and they were married two weeks after the doctor confirmed the pregnancy. Laney finished her sophomore year, but delayed finishing her degree until Dee started school.

She had to admit the first years of the marriage were good. They were young, in love, and full of big plans. They were both smart when it came to money and always lived below their means, stashing the excess for the future. She had just completed her MBA and successfully passed her CPA exam when Greg suggested they buy an ailing fitness club that was in foreclosure. She did the due diligence and agreed it was worth taking the chance. Dee had just started junior high when they opened the doors of their first Bodies for Life. Two years later they opened a second location in a new building and the year after that, they built a new facility for their original club, selling the old building and location to a developer for more than they had originally paid. Now they had three locations, plenty of money in the bank, and an extremely generous offer from an out-of-state company who wanted to add to its own string of clubs.

Their professional life had always been golden, but unfortunately, their personal one had begun to tarnish about the time Dee entered high school. It was the little things at first, forgetting special days, going for days— sometimes weeks—without sex because they were too tired or too busy, the general taking-each-other-for-granted that often happens with couples as they grow used to each other. It's only later, when the damage is done, that the realization hits that the little things were never little. Like small holes that allow the water in, the little things erode the bedrock of a relationship until it collapses.

She had admitted to herself long ago that she had been as guilty of neglect as Greg, but she hadn't been the one to start looking for attention elsewhere. Would he have been faithful if she had made more of an effort to be the girl he had married even though he had long since stopped acting like the man who had been waiting for her at the end of the aisle? Maybe. But wasn't marriage supposed to weather the good times, the bad times, and even the dull times?

She had suspected Greg was cheating for two years before she finally caught him with the manager of a restaurant located next door to one of their clubs. She had been hurt, but willing to go to marriage counseling to try and work things out, but Greg had said no. He wanted a divorce, not because he was in love with his latest fling, but because he felt "stifled" in their marriage and wanted his freedom. Truth be told, that had hurt worse than his infidelity. The divorce had been final for three years, she had been fully recovered for the last two and a half, and now the idiot thought he could win her back.

She pushed away from the door, her racing libido cooled. Thoughts of Greg had that effect nowadays. It looked like she wouldn't need a cold shower after all.

In her bedroom, she undressed and critically examined her naked body in the full-length mirror on the walnut stand in the corner. She had to admit she looked pretty good for a forty-one year old woman. Her weight was the same as it had been when she graduated high school so she didn't have the sag from having gained and lost weight like many of the women who came to Bodies to get firm. Her breasts were on the smallish side, which, of course, she had hated when she was young, but recognized were a benefit as the years passed and she saw gravity taking its toll on her larger-breasted friends. Her buttocks were tight, her legs and arms muscled, and her belly flat thanks to almost daily workouts of one muscle group or another.

Her face looked pretty good, too. Again, no sag due to weight cycling and her skin and eyes had the healthy glow of a woman who took care of herself. She had found a few gray hairs amongst the dark brown ones, but nothing too noticeable yet. Besides, gray hair was why God invented hair dye.

No, she didn't think it was vain to admit that she was an attractive forty-one year old woman, but she did think it was both vain and foolish to think a thirty-year old hunk would be attracted to her. His playful attentions were flattering, but that's all they were—playful. As long as she kept that foremost in her mind, she could relax and enjoy the attention.

She pulled on a nightshirt, brushed her teeth, removed her makeup and gave her shoulder-length curly brown hair a few strokes of the brush before she crawled into bed. She fell asleep quickly, refusing to think of either Greg or the boy next door.

Chapter 2

"Another multi-grain bagel! You make me feel *so* ashamed of myself!"

Greta looked anything but ashamed as she chomped down on her cinnamon roll, the warm icing oozing over her fingers. Between that and her cinnamon dolce latte, Laney estimated Greta had exceeded her recommended sugar allowance for the week.

They were sitting at a corner table in the Rosedale Mall's Starbucks. Greta Crawford, her best friend since their glory days as cheerleaders at Westhaven High, had texted as Laney was getting out of the shower. Starbucks in the morning was their routine whenever Laney was working at the Rosedale Bodies. After gorging on Starbucks sugar, Greta usually assuaged her guilt by working out vigorously at the club. The formula was apparently successful since Greta carried no excess flesh on her six-foot tall body.

"So Greg's not letting up?" Greta licked the icing off her fingers.

"No, he's not, and he's getting on my last nerve. Once this sale is final, I'm going to tell him that if he keeps bothering me, I'll get a restraining order on him."

"He hasn't gotten physical, has he?" Greta stopped eating. "I'll kick his ass for him if he lays a finger on you."

"I might take you up on that if he pins me into a corner one more time and tries to kiss me," Laney said.

"You're kidding! He did that? When and where?"

"At the downtown club yesterday. He smelled like he'd drank his lunch, but that's no excuse. I mean, he wasn't obviously drunk or anything. We were in the office and he started his pitch about getting back together. I got up to leave—it's a little hard to concentrate on payroll when someone's blabbering at you—and that's when he did it."

"Did you knee him in the nuts?"

Laney laughed. "No, Greta, I left his bits and pieces intact. I pushed him away and got out of there— got on a treadmill and jogged until I saw him leave."

She shook her head.

"I don't know what's gotten into him. At first it was kind of flattering, you know. I mean, what woman wouldn't want the man who dumped her to realize what he'd lost? I didn't encourage it, but I kind of enjoyed it. But now it's just getting old."

"Have you told Dee?"

"Of course not. She's been at college. She doesn't need to know her dad is making a fool of himself."

"How long before the sale is final and you can be rid of that idiot for good?"

"We should sign the papers in a few weeks unless the buyer's accountants find something they don't like. I finished the internal audit of the downtown and Spring Valley clubs and sent all our records to the attorneys. The buyer's people are going over those now. I should finish Rosedale's today—or Monday at the latest. I've always been careful to keep everything in order, so the process should go quickly."

"Any news yet on who the buyers are?"

"We still only know the business name—American Fitness, Inc. They've been buying up clubs all over the country. They're privately owned, but we've only met with the attorneys." Laney finished off her black coffee and checked her watch. "I'd better get going. I need to get some work done."

"Oh, I didn't tell you, did I?" Laney said, as they exited Starbucks. "Remember the Davidsons?"

"Sure, that nice old couple who has the house next door to you."

"Their grandson is in town getting the place ready to list. He's going to stop by the club today. I told him I'd get him some guest passes so he can work out while he's here."

"Little Brycie? You're kidding! What's he doing now?"

"I don't think he's doing much. He told me he's a massage therapist, but it sounded like he's not working at the present. He said his grandfather, Ed, passed away a few weeks ago from lung cancer. Doris, his grandmother, is doing well, though."

"I remember his grandpa and grandma as being really nice people. His mom, too. What was her name?"

"Linda. He said she's a nurse practitioner midwife now and has been remarried to a nice man for the last ten years."

"Those days seem like yesterday, don't they?" Greta shook her head. "Guess we're getting old, huh?"

"Remember what I always say. . . ."

"I know, I know. Birthdays are good for you—the more you have, the longer you live."

They separated at the Bodies check-in desk, Greta heading for the women's locker room, Laney for the office on the second-floor loft.

It was a little before ten when the intercom chime on her phone sounded. It was the front desk.

"There's a man here to see you." Patti sounded a little breathless, and Laney had a pretty good idea why.

"I'll be right down," she said.

Bryce was leaning on the desk perusing a brochure, a backpack hanging from one shoulder, seemingly oblivious to the admiring looks cast his way by Patti, three other female employees, and one male employee Laney knew was gay. He was dressed in a lightweight long-sleeve blue plaid shirt with the sleeves rolled up to his elbows, the top three buttons undone, and skintight worn jeans with a rather interesting bulge in the center that Laney tried without success to ignore. When he saw her approaching, he replaced the brochure in the rack and straightened up, smiling.

"Hey, there." He took her by both shoulders and gave her a quick kiss on the cheek. If she wasn't mistaken, Patti was starting to drool.

"Good morning," she said, trying to sound businesslike. God, he smelled good!

She reached into the pocket of her suit jacket and took out a half-dozen guest passes. She held them out to him.

"Six to get you started," she said. "If you're here long enough to need more, just ask."

"Thanks," he said. "Do I get a tour from the owner?"

Laney gave him a quick tour of the facilities. Whether in the close confines of the hall leading to the men's locker room or the spacious room containing the workout machines, Bryce always seemed too close, too "in" her personal space. It wasn't anything she could call him out on, but it was close enough to make her way more aware of his body than she wanted to be. Once they had to step back to allow some people to pass and he put his hand on her back as if to steady her. When he removed it, it felt as if he'd left an imprint of his palm and fingers, an imprint that radiated heat.

Their last stop on the short tour was the juice bar. Greta was perched on a stool at the end. When she saw Bryce, her eyes widened. She looked him up and down, not bothering to hide her interest.

"New member?" she said without looking at Laney.

"This is Bryce Adams, Greta," Laney said. "Remember I told you he was stopping in today?"

Greta glanced at her in surprise before looking back at Bryce.

"Little Brycie?" she said. "Well, now. Haven't you grown up!"

He laughed. "Little Brycie. I haven't heard that in a while."

"I don't imagine you have," Greta said. "You were an adorable little boy, but like the song says, 'Baby, look at you now!'"

"Greta!" Laney was embarrassed. Bryce was smiling, obviously enjoying the attention.

"Hey, facts are facts," Greta said. She turned back to Bryce. "And to think my best friend used to babysit you."

"I was a lucky kid," Bryce said. He extended his arm across Laney's shoulders and pulled her to him. "I loved cuddling on this woman's lap while she read me a story."

"You are incorrigible," Laney muttered, shaking her head. She tried to pull away, but he tightened his grip.

"Of course, my favorite part of our time together was when she gave me a bath."

"Oh, my God!" Greta picked up a napkin and started fanning herself.

"Will you stop!" Laney pushed Bryce away, but couldn't stop herself from laughing. "Go use one of those passes I gave you. I need to get back to work."

"Okay, okay." He raised his hands in mock surrender. "Nice to see you again, Greta."

He turned to go, then stopped and looked back at Laney. "Should I call you when I'm ready to get in the shower?"

"Go!" She picked up a napkin and threw it at him. He winked and walked through the door in the direction of the locker room.

"He is *gorgeous*! I can't believe what a hunk little Brycie grew up to be!" Greta watched his retreating butt until he passed out of sight down the hall to the locker rooms before she turned to Laney. "And he's got the hots big-time for you."

"Don't be ridiculous," Laney said. "He's just joking around."

"Uh, hello? I know you've been out of circulation for a while, but surely, you're not that clueless. The man's wearing his hard-on on his sleeve!"

"You do have a way with words, Greta."

"Just calling it like I see it. He wants you and he wants you bad."

"I'm almost old enough to be his mother."

"You are not. Let's see—you were fifteen when you started sitting him, and he was, what, four? That's only an eleven-year difference. Lots of men have girlfriends or wives eleven years younger than them."

"It's different for men."

"Not anymore. Cougars are the 'in' thing now."

"Well, I'm not a cougar. Besides, Bryce is just fooling around. He's not serious about any of it."

"You think so? Give him an opening and see how serious he is." She leaned closer. "And call me the next day with *all* the yummy details, please."

"Going back to work now," Laney said and started for the door, smiling in spite of herself.

"Details, remember. First dibs on the details," Greta called after her.

Back in her office, Laney pushed all thoughts of Bryce and Greta out of her mind and got back to work. She had always been able to lose herself in numbers. What most people found boring, she found to be almost a form of mediation—a way to focus her mind to the exclusion of everything else.

It was a little after twelve when she heard a knock at her door. She looked up as it opened and Bryce stuck his head in, obviously ignoring the sign on the door that said Employees Only.

"Ready for that lunch?" he said.

Laney started to point the sign out to him, but decided to let it go. She'd only known the adult Bryce since the previous evening, but that had been long enough for her to make an educated guess that he would just try to charm his way out of any rebuke. He wasn't going to be in town that long so what was the point in verbally sparring with him. Besides, it wasn't as if there was anything of great value in the room—and even if there had been, she didn't think he was a thief.

She couldn't help but notice Patti's envious glance as she passed the reception desk. Greta was nowhere to be seen, having apparently left for the day. As they approached the front door, Bryce stepped to the side and held it open with his right hand, positioning himself so that she had to brush close to him to exit. He placed his left hand on her back in the possessive way men unconsciously adopt with their women—except Laney doubted very much that it was unconscious with Bryce.

"I noticed a place a block down that looks good," he said. "The Moonglow Café. How's their food?"

The Moonglow had great food, but it was the last place Laney wanted to go for lunch. It had low lighting, soft booths with high backs for privacy, a liquor license, and an intimate atmosphere. She looked at Bryce suspiciously, wondering if he had scoped it out before coming to the club and knew exactly what it was. But, no, he couldn't have. He had gotten to the club before the Moonglow would have opened.

"The food's not bad," she said. "But their service is slow and I do need to get some work done today. How about Applebee's?"

There was an Applebee's at the front of the Rosedale Mall's parking lot. It was well-lit, noisy, and crowded at lunch—in other words, the perfect place for two people to have a casual lunch with *no* suggestion of intimacy.

He shrugged his acceptance. As they walked across the lot, Bryce kept his hand on her back. She sped up, hoping to get far enough ahead of him that he would have to stop touching her, but he matched her speed.

She knew that they looked like a couple to the shoppers getting out of their cars or driving past, and her face flamed. What must people think, she thought, a woman my age with a man almost young enough to be her son? Then it occurred to her that maybe they did think she was his mother and he was just being an attentive child. Suddenly she felt worse.

The hostess came to attention when they walked through the door, her eyes sliding past Laney as if she didn't exist and focusing on Bryce.

"How many?" she asked.

Can't she count, Laney thought irritably. Maybe if she stopped ogling Bryce long enough, she could see they were the only two in their party.

"Two," Bryce said, his hand still resting on her back. He seemed oblivious to the girl's attention.

Laney breathed a sigh of relief when their waiter turned out to be male. He showed no reaction to Bryce and gave Laney equal attention. Male *and* heterosexual—maybe her lunch order wouldn't get screwed up. After he walked away, Laney turned back to find Bryce watching her, a funny smile on his face.

"What?" she said.

"Just thinking."

"About what?"

"You sure you want to know?" He shifted in his chair as if his jeans had suddenly gotten too tight.

"Never mind," she said, deciding the wisest course of action was to change the subject. "So—I bet you miss California. This town must seem pretty dull to you."

"Not at all," he said. "At least not since I discovered you still live next door."

"I moved back after Greg and I split," Laney said. "We lived across town. He bought out my half of the house. My parents retired about the same time and decided they wanted to move to Florida, so I bought the house from them."

"Boyfriend?"

She shook her head.

"Are the men in this town crazy? First, your husband lets you go, then no one steps up to take his place?"

"I've been too busy for that." Laney felt defensive. She wanted to tell him that, of course, she'd had men ask her out, lots of them, but she'd preferred to avoid the entanglement of relationships. Instead, she started to change the subject to something—anything—that wasn't personal, but before she could, he spoke again.

"Too busy or just afraid to take a chance on someone else?" Bryce wasn't smiling now. "I get the impression that your ex did a number on you."

"I give that impression?" She was surprised. Surely she didn't look like a damaged and pitiful woman to everyone.

He leaned forward, all traces of the flirty, charming lady-killer gone.

"You are a beautiful and very sexy woman, Laney. Yet you don't even notice the looks men give you when you walk by."

"They don't. . . ."

"Oh, yeah, they do." Bryce gestured toward the tables in the bar area, most of them occupied by groups of men on their lunch break. "I saw the heads swiveling when we came in. I'm the envy of every straight guy in the place."

Laney stared at him, speechless. The woman he was describing certainly wasn't her. Sure, she was attractive for her age, but she wasn't some sexpot who made heads "swivel."

"So," he continued. "I know you've had plenty of offers from men. If you didn't, then every man in this town is either gay or crazy, and that's statistically improbable. You've turned them down or discouraged them from asking, both of which are signs of a woman who has been hurt and is afraid she'll be again."

"I thought you said you were a massage therapist, not a psychoanalyst."

What was it with this guy? Why couldn't the big Brycie be more like the little Brycie—just a sweet friendly neighbor kid instead of this person who kept invading her personal space, both physical and emotional?

He laughed.

"Okay, I'll drop it. But before I do, I just have one more thing to say." He turned serious again. "Not all men are like your ex. Some guys mean what they say. Some guys are dependable. Some guys are looking for a woman they can love for the rest of their lives, and if and when they find that woman, they will treasure her and never hurt her."

"You had the barbecued chicken breast?"

The waiter had approached with their food without either of them being aware of it. Laney wanted to jump up and kiss him for sparing her from having to reply to Bryce, but instead she nodded. He set her plate down and placed the burger and fries in front of Bryce.

"Can I get you anything else?"

They both shook their heads. For the next several minutes, neither of them spoke, concentrating all their attention on their food.

"Almost forgot to tell you," Bryce said, his tone light again. "Talked to Mom last night. She was really surprised to hear you were still living next door. She said to tell you 'hello.' "

"Tell her the same from me when you speak to her again," Laney said, relieved at the change of subject.

"She asked me if you were still as pretty as you were back then," he said. "When I told her you looked even better, she said, uh-oh, guess I won't be seeing my boy for a while."

Laney shook her head, laughing.

"I bet the California women don't stand a chance when you turn on the charm, do they?"

"Charm? I don't know what you mean." His leg bumped against hers under the table and stayed there. She pulled hers back quickly.

"So, do you have a girlfriend?" she asked and immediately wanted to bite her tongue. He would see the question as a sign of interest on her part when all she really wanted to do was shift attention from herself.

"Nope. Nothing serious. I do date—unlike you—but I haven't found anyone I wanted to be permanently involved with. And, like you, I stay pretty busy with work."

"I thought you weren't working now."

"What gave you that idea?"

"Well, when I asked you what you do, it sounded like you were between jobs."

"No, I'm working. Just took some time to come back and take care of business here is all." He grinned. "Back to your girlfriend question. Why do you ask?"

"Just making conversation, Bryce. Don't read anything into it." She was starting to feel in control of herself again. The guy had the unnerving ability to make her feel like a silly sex-starved teenager, but she reminded herself she was a professional woman with a successful business and an ordered life.

"Damn! I was hoping you were checking to see if I was available."

"Let's talk about the weather."

He burst out laughing. "Okay, okay, I'll drop it. Doesn't mean I'm going to give up, though."

They spent the remainder of the meal in light conversation, talking about how the town had changed in the years he'd been gone. He tried to pick up the check, but she insisted on paying her share and on leaving the tip.

It was almost one and most of the lunch crowd had cleared out. As they approached the inner front door of the restaurant, Bryce stepped ahead as he had at the club, holding the door open with his right hand while possessively pressing his left hand against her back. She had just started to step through when she came face-to-face with her ex-husband.

Greg was with two other men whose faces were familiar to her. She thought they were regulars at the downtown club. When Greg saw her, he started to smile in welcome before he registered Bryce at her side.

"Laney," he said, glancing back and forth between the two of them. "I didn't realize you were working Rosedale today. "

"Hello, Greg," she said.

Greg motioned to the other men to go ahead. "Grab a table. I'll be there in a minute."

"Greg Mitchell," he said, extending his right hand to Bryce. "I don't believe I've had the pleasure."

"Bryce Adams," Bryce said, shaking Greg's hand.

The three of them stepped back and to the side of the hostess area so as not to block incoming patrons. Bryce positioned himself close to Laney's side, his left hand still resting on her back in that possessive way he had. Laney could see from the expression in Greg's green eyes that he had picked up on the body language. Good, she thought, staying put instead of moving away from Bryce's touch. Let him think something is going on even though nothing is. Maybe that will make him leave me alone.

"Bryce is Doris and Ed Davidson's grandson," Laney said. "He's in town to get their house ready to list."

"You're staying next door?" Laney almost laughed at Greg's expression.

"Sure am," Bryce said. "Laney's been showing me around. We have a lot of catching up to do."

"You know each other?"

"Laney was my babysitter when my mother and I lived with my grandparents," Bryce said. "My *favorite* babysitter, I might add."

He slid his hand up to her shoulder and draped his arm casually around her.

"We need to get going," Laney said, making a point of glancing at her watch. "I need to get back to work."

"Sure, sure," Greg said, stepping back. "Same here. Nice meeting you, Mr. Adams."

"Nice meeting you, too, Greg," he said. "It gives me a chance to thank you."

"Thank me?" Greg was puzzled. "For what?"

"For being a fool and setting this woman free," Bryce said. "I really appreciate it."

Greg's mouth opened, but nothing came out. Bryce winked at him, pushed the door open with his right hand, and with his left arm still around Laney's shoulders, escorted her out of the restaurant.

"You didn't just do that!" Laney stopped at the corner of the building, out of sight of the restaurant's windows. "I can't believe you just did that!"

Bryce laughed. "Hey, admit it. Didn't you enjoy the look on his face just a little bit?"

Laney stared at him for a minute, then burst out laughing.

"Okay, okay. I enjoyed it. A lot. Maybe now he'll back off."

"Back off?"

"He's been after me to get back together," Laney said. "I've told him repeatedly that's not going to happen, but he just doesn't let up."

"Guess he's not quite the fool I thought he was," Bryce said. "At least he's smart enough to know he screwed up when he let you go."

They started walking back across the lot toward Bodies. Bryce had dropped his hand down to her back again, but in case Greg was looking out the window, Laney didn't try to move away from him. Besides, it felt kind of nice.

"It's difficult to avoid him while we're still business partners," Laney said. "Once the sale is final, though. . . ."

"Won't he just have more free time to pursue you?"

"If he does, I'll get a restraining order," Laney said. "I'm getting sick of it."

"I'm glad to hear you feel that way."

Laney chose not to ask him to elaborate on *that* statement. She had a pretty good idea what he would say.

In her office, Bryce picked up his backpack and slung it over one shoulder.

"How about showing me the town tonight?" he said.

"I can't."

"Hey, it's Friday and you already said you don't have a date. Let's get a start on the weekend."

"I've got a lot I need to do at home," Laney said. "The grass needs mowing, I need to catch up on my laundry, and I'll probably have to come in and do some more on the books tomorrow so I need to get to bed at a decent hour. I want to finish this audit. I want the sale to go through as quickly as possible."

"I second that," Bryce said. "But you still need to eat."

"I'll just order a pizza and get started on stuff around the house. But thanks anyway."

"Where's the best pizza place in town?" he asked. "I may need to make use of delivery myself while I'm here."

"I like Peppino's. It's locally owned, not a chain, and they make their own dough."

"Good to know," he said.

"It was really nice having lunch with you," she said. "Maybe I'll see you again before you leave."

She started to turn toward her desk, but Bryce reached out, took her arm and pulled her gently to him. Putting the tip of a finger under her chin, he tilted her head up.

"I have a question," he said.

"What's that?" Laney knew she should move back from him, but she stayed where she was.

"I don't plan on giving up," he said. He moved his fingers lightly over her face, brushing her hair back from her cheek. His lips curled up to one side in that cute way he had. "Are you going to get a restraining order on me?"

"Now you're being silly," she said and looked away from him, laughing. "You're just trying to make me feel good."

"Oh, I would very much like to make you feel good," he said, his voice lowering.

"Bryce . . . ," She started to pull away, but he stopped her, sliding his hand around to the back of her neck.

"Thanks for going to lunch with me," he mumbled as his lips lightly touched hers. Then he was gone, the office door shutting behind him.

Laney stood rooted to the spot, unable to move or think. The touch of his hand on her back and his leg against hers under the table at Applebee's, the way he had of looking at her, his constant innuendos, and the way he had held her so possessively in front of Greg had all been ratcheting up her libido bit by bit over the course of the last hour. The touch of his lips to hers had just sent it through the roof! She'd thought she was over all that for good, that she would be content to live out the rest of her days alone, but Bryce had lit a fire that she was afraid she might not be able to put out.

"I should never have taken that damn babysitting job!" she muttered through clenched teeth and turned to her desk, determined to put Bryce, Greg, and sex out of her mind. It took the better part of an hour before she succeeded.

Chapter 3

The smell of freshly mowed grass greeted Laney as she stepped out of her car. Uniform stripes and trimmed edges graced her front lawn, compliments she was sure of the "boy" next door. She knew she should go over and demand he stop doing things like this, but she was too grateful that the work was done. It had been a long day, and she hadn't been looking forward to coming home to yard work. She decided to strike a happy medium. She wouldn't yell at him, but she wouldn't thank him either.

The back yard looked as perfect as the front. Laney poured herself a glass of wine and stood looking out her patio doors. It had been a long time since a man had helped her with anything around the house. Not just since the divorce—she had not let any man into her life in the last three years so that was on her. But even before, when she and Greg were still together, she had done all of the cleaning and most of the yard work. They occasionally hired a neighborhood kid to mow, but she had often done it herself. Greg preferred nice suits and manicures to jeans and calloused hands. Oh, he kept himself in great shape, of course, but he preferred accomplishing that through regular workouts at Bodies rather than through hard work. His body was lean and strong, but it was only for show, not for hard use.

She finished her wine, rinsed the glass, and set it on the counter by the sink in case she wanted a second one later. She changed from her pantsuit and into a pair of old jeans and a red tee. She sorted her laundry into three piles, dropping the whites and light colors into the washer first. Plugging in the vacuum, she gave the house a quick pass, thankful again that it was small and only one-story. Why did everyone want a big house nowadays? Big houses meant more work, as well as more expense. This house with its one bath had been plenty big enough for her and her parents when she was growing up, and it was more than big enough for her now.

She had just poured herself a second glass of wine and was thinking about calling Peppino's when the doorbell rang. She wasn't expecting any visitors, but she had a pretty good idea it was her new "yard boy" at the door. Just like a man, she thought. Does you a favor, then makes himself available so you can show your gratitude. Well, he wasn't going to get it from her no matter how cute his grin.

"Pizza boy," Bryce said when she opened the door. He was holding a flat cardboard box with the Peppino's logo on top. Her stomach growled as the aroma hit her nostrils.

"Bryce . . . ," she started to protest, but he held up his hand.

"Hey, all I'm doing is delivering. I know you have a lot to do. Just thought I'd help you out a little by dropping this off."

"It's probably not even the kind I like," she said, knowing she sounded like a petulant child.

"According to Ricky, it is," he said. Ricky Smith was one of the regular evening employees at Peppino's.

"I figured since Peppino's is your favorite, the guys who work there would know what you like."

He held up his right hand, balancing the box on his left palm.

"Let's see—onions, pepperoni, olives, and mushrooms? Right?"

She nodded reluctantly. "Yes, that's what I usually get."

"Well, then, there you go." He thrust the box at her.

She took the pizza and stepped back. "Hold on a minute and I'll get my purse."

"No, you won't. It's my treat. Later." He turned to go.

"Did you mow my grass?" The wayward tongue again! She should have bitten it off at lunch! She had already decided not to say anything to him about the grass, but here she was blurting it out almost the minute she saw him.

"No big deal," he said. "I was mowing Grandma's and thought I might as well do yours while I was at it."

"Well . . . ," Laney started, then thought, oh, what the hell. "Thank you. But you really didn't need to do that."

"I know."

"It does look nice." She looked at the yard. "I never bother to stripe it like that, but it does look good."

"I had a yard business when I was in high school," he said. "I learned early on that striping it like that got me a lot more customers than the kids who didn't stripe."

She stood there for a second before letting out an exasperated sigh.

"Oh, come on in," she said, stepping back from the door. "The least I can do is share the pizza."

"Gee, don't mind if I do."

He grinned that lopsided grin again, and Laney knew she'd been played. Mow the lawn, deliver her favorite pizza—a large, if the box was any indication, meaning he fully expected to be invited to share it—and he'd be in like Flynn.

Was there no end to his persistence, she wondered? Bryce had been correct in assuming she'd been asked out more than once since she and Greg had split. She had politely turned down the offers, and for the most part, that had been it. Oh, one or two guys had asked again, but when she hadn't budged, they gave up and moved on to greener pastures. Bryce, on the other hand, seemed determined to insert himself into her life whether she liked it or not.

The uncomfortable part was admitting to herself that she did like it just a little bit. Having a young, handsome, and very sexy man pursuing you was a major ego booster, of course, but it was more than that. His attentions were starting to awaken something in her that she'd thought was asleep for good. She hadn't decided yet whether that was a good thing or a bad thing.

"I was having a glass of wine." She set the pizza box on the counter-height tavern table that stood in the middle of her kitchen. "I have beer as well, if you prefer that."

"Beer sounds good," Bryce said as he plopped down on one of the four stools.

Laney opened a bottle of Michelob and placed it on the table, followed by two salad plates and napkins. "Do you need a fork or salt?" she asked.

"Nope," he said. "Pizza was made to be eaten with hands, and it doesn't need salt."

He opened the box and lifted a piece to her plate, then one to his own. They ate without talking for a few minutes. Somewhere down the street, a lawnmower sputtered to life, and in the yard backing up to Laney's, a dog barked. She sipped her wine and chewed her pizza and began to relax.

"How's the book work coming?" Bryce asked, helping himself to a second piece.

"Almost done," she said. "It shouldn't take more than another day."

"Then what happens?"

"Then the buyer's accountants go over them," she said. "They already have the books from our other two locations. Greg told me a few days ago that they've finished their audit of the downtown location and are more than halfway through Spring Valley's."

"Everything looks good then?"

She nodded. "I've always been careful to keep the books in order. There shouldn't be any problems from that end."

"So when do you expect the sale to be final?"

"Within the month," she said. "Certainly before the Fourth anyway."

"What are your plans then?"

"I really don't have any," she said. "I'm looking forward to not having to work at anything, but I suspect it will only be a few weeks before I go stir crazy. Since my junior year of high school, the only time I haven't had a job was right after Dee was born. I took a year off, then went back to part-time work until she started school. After that I went back to college—I had dropped out when I found out I was pregnant. We bought the clubs shortly after and I've been working ever since."

"You sound like you're good at what you do," he said. "I'm sure a lot of companies would jump at the chance to hire you."

She shook her head. "I don't know. It's been a long time since I've had to do the whole job-hunting thing. I don't even have a resume."

"Easy enough to make one," he said. "But will you have to work? Won't you get enough from the sale that you won't have to do anything else?"

"Well, yes, we will," she said. "Money won't be an issue. Boredom will."

He nodded. "I get that. Hey, change of subject. I've got a favor to ask."

Uh-oh, she thought. Now what?

"I thought I'd pick out paint and carpet for the house this weekend, but I'm terrible at that kind of thing." He glanced around. "Your place looks great. You seem to know how to put colors together, so how about going shopping with me tomorrow?"

He had one of those helpless-around-the-house looks that men had perfected to an art form to avoid all those tedious chores that fell under the blanket label of "women's work." Laney had no doubt he could get any help he needed from the salespeople at the local Lowe's, but he'd chosen to ask her. The innocuousness of the request made it difficult to say no, but she couldn't shake the feeling that she was being played again.

"I need to put in a few hours at the club in the morning," she said, delaying having to answer.

"Afternoon is fine," he said. "I've got some things to take care of in the A.M. myself. How about I pick you up at the club at noon?"

Laney busied herself with getting another slice of pizza from the box, trying to think of a graceful way to get out of spending Saturday afternoon shopping for paint and carpet with him. She took a bite, chewed, and finally gave up.

"Noon is fine," she said.

"Great. We'll get lunch, then hit the stores." He grinned that lopsided grin. "It will be fun. We can pretend we're newlyweds fixing up our first house."

"I don't think so," she said, trying to look stern, but before she knew it, she was smiling back at him.

She cleaned off the table when they were finished, wrapping the three remaining slices of pizza in a piece of foil. She placed it in front of him.

"Your breakfast," she said.

He chuckled. "Just like college."

"You went to college?" she said.

"You sound surprised."

"Well, you said you were a massage therapist. I just thought you had gone to school for that and nothing else."

"Did that after UCLA," he said. "I took some classes while still in high school, so that made me a sophomore when I started college. I took full loads and went full-time in the summer and got my degree by the time I was twenty."

Laney was impressed and said so.

"What was your major?"

"Pre-med." He chuckled at her shocked expression. "Yeah, I know. Doesn't fit me, right? That's what I decided, too. The more I looked at medicine, the more I decided I didn't want to be on that end of the health spectrum, fixing things after they were broken. I wanted to prevent the problems in the first place. So I went into massage therapy. Nothing like it for relieving stress and pain."

His eyes drifted down over her body, then back up to her face.

"Would you like me to show you?"

The thought of his hands on her body brought a flush of warmth that started in her groin and spread both directions. She knew he could see the flush in her face, but couldn't do anything about it.

"I'm relaxed enough," she said, turning to the sink. She began rinsing the plates. "Thank you anyway."

"I don't know. You look awfully tense to me."

He had come up behind her and was standing close. She hadn't heard him get off the stool. Suddenly she felt his hands on her shoulders. They began to knead, lightly at first, then pressed deeper.

"Just as I thought," he said, his voice low. "You've got a lot of knots in there. You really ought to let me work them out. I don't have a table with me, but I'm sure we could make do with your bed."

Oh, my God, Laney thought, as the image of Bryce straddling her in her bed, rubbing every inch of her body exploded in her mind. The warmth that rushed through her made her knees wobble. This had to stop. She was a mature woman and she was getting dangerously close to making a fool of herself over a young stud.

The plate slipped out of her hands, clattering in the sink. She turned, knocking his hands off her shoulders.

"Bryce, please. You have to stop this . . . ," she stopped, realizing the sudden turn had been a mistake. Now they were facing one another, only inches apart. She expected him to have the cute, but cocky, grin on his face, but he wasn't smiling. The look in his eyes was a surprising mixture of lust and tenderness, and for a moment, Laney found herself unable to move or speak.

Then he grinned and the spell was broken.

"Stop what?" he said, stepping back. "I just thought you could use a shoulder massage."

"Well, I don't need one. My shoulders are just fine." Picking up a damp dishrag, she moved away from the sink and Bryce, busying herself with wiping the table. "You really need to go. I've got some things I need to do."

"Sure, no problem." Bryce started towards the door. "Thanks for the beer and pizza."

Laney started to remind him that he had brought the pizza, but nodded instead. She didn't want to prolong the conversation any more than necessary. She just wanted him out of the house and out of her personal space while she still possessed some measure of dignity.

"See you tomorrow."

The door shut behind him before Laney could think of a way to withdraw her consent to help him pick out paint and carpet. Why had she let him trap her into agreeing to that? She didn't know how to handle men like him—or any man, for that matter. She had married young, long before she gained experience with men. Sure, she was forty-one years old, but when it came to men, she had about as much man smarts as a fifteen-year old.

Bryce was playing with her—well, not exactly playing. She had thought it was only kidding at first, but now she was convinced he would bed her in a heartbeat if she gave him the chance. Maybe screwing an older woman—his former babysitter, no less—was on his bucket list. Something to brag to his California buddies about when he returned home, maybe even post on Facebook. She had to stop letting him get to her before she did something she would regret later.

Thinking about him bragging about his conquest helped cool her off. She had to keep that foremost in her mind. If she did, maybe she could deal with him. He would be gone soon. A man like him would soon tire of not getting anywhere, finish what he had to do, and hurry back to his California conquests—of which, she was sure, there were many. She would go with him to choose paint and carpet tomorrow, anything to get him out of town that much faster.

Chapter 4

"You ought to invite your cute neighbor to the pool party tomorrow," Greta said. "I'd love to see him in a pair of swim trunks. Out of a pair of swim trunks would be even better, but I'll leave that to you."

"Will you stop?" Laney glanced around. Starbucks was crowded with people having their caffeine and sugar breakfast, fuel for their Saturday shopping marathon. "Someone is going to hear you."

"Nobody's paying any attention to us." Greta waved her hand at the people around them, most of whom were looking at their smartphones. "They're too busy texting and checking Facebook to bother eavesdropping on us."

"I haven't decided if I'm going tomorrow. Even if I do, I'm not taking Bryce."

"You've got to go," Greta protested. "You know Lee's still in London. You're my date. I don't object to a threesome, though, if you want to bring Bryce."

Lee, Greta's husband, was a partner at one of the largest accounting firms in the country. He was on the road or in the air more than he was home, but he and Greta seemed to have adapted well to being apart so much. Greta said it kept the spark alive. They'd never had children, leaving Greta free to hop on a plane and meet him somewhere exotic at a moment's notice.

"I'm not bringing Bryce. And if you see him, don't you dare mention the party to him."

Joanna and Bill Miller had sent out invitations to their party over a month ago. At Greta's urging, Laney had RSVP'd that she'd attend, but she wasn't looking forward to it. It wasn't that the Millers, both successful attorneys, didn't throw a good party. They lived in a gorgeous home in a gated community just south of town. Each year, usually in early June, they threw a pool party to celebrate the opening of their pool and the unofficial start of summer, hiring the best caterers and a DJ for the evening festivities. The party usually started early afternoon and continued until the sober drivers the Millers hired to transport guests who'd drank too much took the last person home. Greg and Laney had attended every year after they had become acquainted with Joanna and Bill, and Laney had continued to attend after the split. Greg had brought a date the first year, and Laney had left early. He had come alone the last two. They had been polite and civil to one another, and it hadn't been too unpleasant.

Laney knew this year would be different. Greg had decided he wanted her back. With that attitude and the alcohol she knew would be flowing, he would more than likely be a major pain in the butt. She didn't want a scene, and she was afraid that's exactly what would happen.

"Greg will probably be there, Greta. You know how he's been lately."

"Good reason to bring your sexy neighbor," Greta said. "Call it protection."

Laney flashed back to the day before at Applebee's. Bryce would be a buffer between her and Greg, but talk about a scene! She knew how determined Greg could be when he'd been drinking. Put the obstacle of Bryce between him and what he wanted, and the sparks would really fly!

"I don't think that's a good idea," she said. She hadn't told Greta about Applebee's. "It wouldn't be fair to put Bryce in the middle of an unpleasant situation like that."

"I think little Brycie would handle himself just fine."

Oh, he can handle himself, Laney thought. No doubt about that! She had never seen Greg at a loss for words until the day before. But Greg would be ready for Bryce if they met again. While some women might enjoy two men clashing in public over them, the idea mortified Laney.

"Okay, okay, I'll go," she said. "But Bryce is not to know about the party. Understood?"

"If you insist," Greta said, "but I think you're missing the perfect opportunity to knock Greg down a notch or two. You want me to pick you up?"

"No, I'll meet you there." Laney finished her coffee and pushed back from the table. "I need to get going. Bryce got me to agree to go shopping with him this afternoon for paint and carpet, and I need to get some work done first."

Greta's eyebrows rose.

"Shut up," Laney said before she could speak. "I don't want to hear it. It's no big deal. Besides, the faster he gets the work done on the house, the sooner he'll head back to California."

Greta chuckled, and Laney fought the urge to smack her.

***

It was noon on the dot when the reception desk notified her Bryce was waiting. She had worked steadily for several hours, but as it got closer to noon, she'd found it hard to concentrate. In spite of her resolve of the day before, she found herself looking forward to seeing him. She knew she was being a fool, but in his presence, she felt alive and young and desirable—all things she hadn't felt in a long time and hadn't expected to ever feel again. As long as she was careful not to let it go any further, she supposed there wasn't any harm in enjoying those feelings.

Tim, a local high school senior who worked part-time at Bodies, was working the reception desk. He and Bryce were engaged in a lively conversation about baseball. Bryce stopped talking when he saw her approaching the desk, his eyes drifting down over the snug green tee she had chosen because it brought out the green in her hazel eyes. She could almost feel the touch of his gaze on her breasts, and she was suddenly aware of her stretch jeans rubbing her crotch.

"Hey," she said, feeling a little awkward with Tim watching.

"Hey, yourself," Bryce said. He leaned forward and pecked her on the cheek. "You look great."

"Thanks," she said. "Well, I guess we'd better get going."

"Nice meeting you," Bryce said to Tim, who responded with, "You, too."

"Nice kid," Bryce said as they walked to his car in the lot.

"Yes, he is," Laney said.

"So where do you want to get lunch?"

"Any place is fine. Are you going to Lowe's for the carpet and paint, or did you have other stores in mind?"

"I don't know the area, so unless you can recommend some other place, Lowe's it is. I'm in your hands."

She glanced at him to see if the comment was another of his innuendos, but he was looking straight ahead. Maybe he was already tiring of his game—but just then his hand came to rest possessively on her back, and she knew the game was still on.

They stopped for lunch at Panera Bread just down the street from the Lowe's. Laney ordered the Lemon Chicken Orzo soup; Bryce opted for a turkey sandwich and chips. She was expecting lunch to be a repeat of the day before—the innuendos, a knee "accidentally" brushing hers under the table, but he surprised her by sticking to normal conversation and his knees stayed on his side of the table. He seemed interested in hearing about the area. Over the years, he had visited his grandparents four or five times, but only for a week or two at the most. More often they made the trip to California. By the end of the meal, she had relaxed.

"So what do we do first?" he asked as they entered the giant Lowe's store. "Paint or carpet?"

"Let's go to flooring first," she said. "Once you choose that, you can take a sample of it to paint so you can get something that goes with it."

She almost laughed at his expression as he looked at the array of carpet choices facing him.

"This isn't going to be easy, is it?" he said. He turned to her. "Help me out here. What should I get?"

"If it was for a house you were going to live in," she said. "I'd say pick something you really like that fits your budget. But the advice is usually to stay neutral with houses you're getting ready to sell or rent. And don't buy the cheapest or the most expensive either—something midrange price-wise and beige, in other words."

"So, what are you saying? Boring carpet sells a house?"

She laughed.

"Beige isn't boring after people move furniture in and hang drapes and pictures. But it does go with everything and that's what appeals to most buyers."

"And I guess I paint the walls white?"

"Not stark white, but, yeah, an off-white is best. It goes. . . ."

". . . with everything," he finished for her. "I get it. Let's look around a little first."

They spent the next hour fondling carpet samples, admiring ceramic tile and arguing over whether light or dark hardwood floors looked better. The middle-aged man working the department offered his help, but stayed out of their way when he saw they were window-shopping first.

Bryce kept coming back to the ceramic tile. "I really like that one," he said, pointing to cream-colored rough textured tile with streaks of gray and beige. "That would go with everything, wouldn't it?"

"Well, yeah, it would, but tile is more expensive. Most people expect carpet."

"Not in California."

"Probably not, but this isn't California. Tile floors are cold and we do have winter here. No one wants to put their feet on a cold tile floor when they get out of bed on a winter morning."

"Couldn't I just put carpet in the bedrooms and tile everywhere else?"

"I guess you could do that," Laney admitted. "But like I said, it's going to cost you more, and you might not recoup the expense when the house sells."

"Let's go look at paint," Bryce said. "Maybe that will be easier."

An hour later he still hadn't made up his mind.

"Let's get out of here," he said. "I thought this would be quick and simple, but I see I'm going to have to think about it."

His hand rested on her back as they walked to the car. She kept glancing at him, trying to determine if there was any meaning to the touch, but he seemed deep in thought. Maybe touching a woman's back in this way was an automatic thing with him.

"Do you have to get back right away?" he asked when they were back in the car. When she hesitated, he added, "I thought we might drive around for a bit and you could show me the area."

"I guess I could." She didn't have any plans for the rest of the day, and he had behaved himself so far.

"Great!"

They drove around town, Laney pointing out restaurants and historic landmarks and the schools his mother had attended, then headed out of town into the country. It was a perfect day—warm, but with a gentle breeze that offset the sun's heat just enough to be pleasant. They passed several horse farms, admiring the beauty of the long-legged thoroughbreds grazing in the pastures and the ostentatious mansions of their owners. Just before four, they came over a rise and Bryce leaned forward in surprise.

"What the heck—a castle?" he said.

"A castle that's a bed and breakfast," she said. "Ten or so rooms, a restaurant, a tennis court, pool, and rooms for events."

"Not too shabby," Bryce said. "A restaurant, you said? Want to grab dinner?"

Laney laughed. "I don't think we're dressed for it."

"One of those suit and tie places, huh?"

"I'm afraid so. Jeans won't cut it. Besides, I'm pretty sure the restaurant doesn't open this early."

"You've been there?"

"Once—a lot of years ago. Greg and I had dinner with some friends who were moving to Europe. Just dinner, though—we didn't stay there. But I hear it's very nice."

"Looks like it would be."

They headed back toward town, taking their time, enjoying the weather and the scenery. Laney caught herself glancing over at Bryce several times. God, he is gorgeous, she thought. And fun to be around when he wasn't nuzzling her neck or making thinly veiled suggestions that they hop in the sack together. Not that that wouldn't be even more fun than taking a Saturday afternoon drive with him—if she were only eleven years younger. But she wasn't and giving in to that temptation would not only be making a fool of herself, it would likely ruin what could turn out to be a pleasant friendship—at least until he went home.

"How about we stop at a supermarket and pick up something to grill," he said as they stopped at a red light just inside the city limits. "It's too nice of a day to eat inside."

"Oh, I don't know . . . ," she started.

"You're probably busy. Sorry. I wasn't thinking."

"No, it's not that."

"You don't have any plans tonight?"

"No, but. . . ."

"I don't know about you, but I hate to eat alone. So, how about it?"

He looked at her, waiting for her answer, a friendly and perfectly innocent smile on his face. Laney couldn't think of a good reason to object, so she shrugged her shoulders.

"Okay," she said. "I guess we could do that. My grill hasn't been fired up since last fall, but there should still be gas in the tank."

"If there's not, I'll go get some."

As the light changed and they pulled through the intersection, he began humming. Laney stole a look at him. He was grinning that cute little grin again, one side of his lips pulled up. His eyes were on the road, but his peripheral vision must have caught her looking. The grin disappeared, the neutral expression back in place.

He'd done it again! He'd played her and she'd fallen for it. All day he'd been on his best behavior with the friendly neighbor-guy act, knowing it would cause her to lower her defenses. She had expected to spend a couple of hours having lunch and picking out carpet and paint. Instead, she had spent the entire afternoon with him and, to make matters worse, had just agreed to spend the evening with him as well.

Well, maybe she was committed to the dinner portion of it, but she would certainly see to it that he headed home after they'd eaten their steaks or chicken or whatever they decided to grill. To paraphrase a bad

Western, he'd better be out of her back yard before sundown!

Suddenly she felt her lips begin to curve in a smile and she quickly turned as if to look out the window at the stores they were passing. His constant and unwavering pursuit was a real ego boost even if part of her did still suspect he was just trying to add another name to his list of conquests. There were certainly other women in town that he could have homed in on, but instead he finagled ways to spend as much time as he could with her in the hope, no doubt, of wearing down her defenses. It wasn't going to work, of course, but she had to admit she was enjoying the game just a little.

After a few minutes of discussion at Kroger's meat counter, they decided on a steak for him and a chicken breast for her. A container of coleslaw and another of potato salad, a foil-wrapped loaf of garlic bread, a bottle of wine, and a six-pack of Mich Light completed their order. Bryce was friendly to all the clerks, male and female, young and old, and Laney again found herself comparing him to Greg. She'd hated shopping for anything with Greg. He invariably copped an attitude with salespeople, waiters, cashiers—anyone he seemed to feel was put on the earth to serve him. Nothing ever satisfied him. If Greg had been with her, the supermarket employees would have been scowling, instead of smiling and laughing and telling them to have a good time.

Back at the house, Bryce started the grill while Laney sprinkled seasonings on the steak and chicken— garlic salt for the steak and jerk seasoning for the chicken. She set out paper plates, steak knives, forks, napkins, salt, and pepper. With the plate of steak and chicken in one hand and a beer for Bryce tucked under her arm, she slid open the patio door.

"Thanks," he said, twisting the cap off the beer. He took a long swig. "Ah, that's good. Nothing better than a beer on a summer day. Especially when it's in the company of a beautiful woman."

Laney set the plate on the grill's side shelf. "Pay attention to your grill."

"Yes, ma'm." He mock-saluted her, that adorable crooked grin on his face. She turned and hurried back into the house before he could see her starting to smile in response to it.

Safely back inside, she poured herself a glass of wine and stood watching him while she sipped it. He checked the grill's temperature gauge, then placed the steak and the chicken on the grate and closed the cover. His back was to the house as he stood, his left hand in his pocket, his right holding the beer, gazing around the yard. Laney allowed her eyes to wander over the outlines of his body, admiring his broad shoulders and shapely butt. All it would take, she thought, is one word from me. She had little doubt he would give her a night to remember. Just thinking about it made her start to tingle and grow warm, and she moved her hips a little, enjoying the press of her jeans against her suddenly sensitive clitoris. Then she shook herself and set the glass down hard. A few drops of wine sloshed out onto the counter and she dabbed it up with a dishrag.

"Get a grip," she muttered to herself.

No doubt he would show her a great time, but what about the next morning? And the mornings after that? He would go back to California, another notch on his jockstrap, and brag to all his friends about his conquest.

He might even post something on Facebook about the night he spent with his former babysitter. Didn't all young people post or tweet every moment of their lives nowadays? She got on Facebook occasionally to keep up with Dee's life, and was often amazed at the mundane—and sometimes embarrassing—stuff she saw posted there. What if Bryce did that and Dee saw it?

Yet, as she stood there watching Bryce tending the grill, she somehow knew that wasn't his style. He wasn't some silly kid. He was a thirty-year-old man, with "man" being the operative word. If she had to bet, she would bet that he would make wonderful love to her and never speak of it to anyone. But could she take that chance? Even if he didn't broadcast his conquest to the social networking world, he would still go back to California. There wasn't any future for them.

Greg had been her first and only lover. Was she capable of having a meaningless fling for the sake of sex? She admitted to herself for the first time that one of the reasons—maybe the main reason—she had turned down date offers in the years since the divorce was because she wasn't sure how to handle the sexual aspect of dating. What about the danger of diseases and pregnancy? She wasn't on the pill. She and Greg had decided one child was enough—actually Greg had decided—and he'd gotten a vasectomy. She'd never had any reason to concern herself with contraceptive measures. She wasn't even sure if she was any good in bed. Maybe she should get some books and read up on it. . . .

"Meat's about ready," Bryce called over his shoulder.

She shook herself out of her crazy thoughts, grabbed the foil-wrapped loaf of garlic bread and took it out to the grill to warm while the steak and chicken finished cooking.

***

They had just finished eating and were kicked back in the Adirondack chairs enjoying the beautiful weather and the satisfaction that comes with a good meal when the front door slammed. Laney sat up, alarmed. She was sure she had locked the door when she left this morning. She and Bryce had come in through the garage, so it should still be locked.

"Mom?"

A moment later the patio doors slid open.

"Hey?" Dee said, a question mark in her voice when she saw Bryce.

Laney had jumped to her feet when she'd heard Dee call out, feeling herself start to flush. She felt like the kid instead of the mother, a kid who had just been caught with a boy in the house when the parents were gone.

"Dee! I didn't expect you home. What happened to your trip?"

"Jana got food poisoning. She's over the worst part, but we decided to postpone it for a week until she's feeling better."

Bryce had gotten to his feet, his nearly empty second beer in his hand, when Dee stepped onto the patio. Laney noticed her daughter's eyes widen briefly as they swept over him. Dee ran a hand over her short blond hair, smoothing it. She stood straighter, her breasts thrusting out in the unconscious response of a female to an attractive male. Yes, honey, Laney thought. He has that effect on every woman.

"Bryce, this is my daughter, Deanna. Dee, this is Bryce Adams. His grandparents are the Davidsons."

Bryce stepped forward, offering his hand to Dee. She shook it, her face flushing slightly when their hands touched.

"Bryce is in town to get the house ready to list for sale," Laney said. "I think I've told you before about babysitting a little boy who lived next door. That was Bryce."

"Oh, wow!" Dee said. "Mom was your babysitter?"

"My favorite babysitter," Bryce said.

Laney said a silent prayer that he wouldn't mention bath time to her daughter like he had to Greta. He glanced over at Laney, that crooked grin on his face, and she knew he knew what she was thinking.

"Are you hungry?" Laney asked. "There's some ground turkey patties in the freezer. It wouldn't take long to thaw one in the microwave and grill it, and there's plenty of slaw and potato salad left."

"I ate. Vic and I stopped at Friday's after we dropped Jana off." She looked back at Bryce. "So you guys were just hanging out?"

"Your mom went to Lowe's with me today to look at carpet and paint." Bryce gestured toward the house on the other side of the privacy fence. "I need to fix the place up a little before I put it on the market, and I know nothing about picking out carpet and paint. I figured the least I could do was cook her a meal as a thank you."

He set the empty beer bottle on the grill's side shelf.

"I'll get out of here. You two haven't seen one another in a while and you probably have a lot to talk about."

"You don't have to go," Dee said at the same time that Laney said, "Maybe we'll see you again before you go home."

Bryce looked from one to the other, smiling. His gaze lingered on Laney, the twinkle in his eyes indicating he was enjoying her discomfort.

"No, really," he said to Dee. "I do need to get home. I've got a few things I need to do."

"Well, okay," Dee said, obviously disappointed. "Hey, I've got an idea."

She turned to Laney.

"We're going to the Millers tomorrow, right?"

Oh, crap, Laney thought. Before she could reply, Dee turned to Bryce.

"The Millers are friends of ours. Every summer they throw a fantastic pool opening party. It starts in the afternoon and goes way into the night. Why don't you come with us?"

"I'm sure Bryce has things to do," Laney tried, but Bryce was nodding his head.

"Sure, I'd love to." He turned to Laney, that infuriating grin on his face. "As long as it's okay with your mom."

"Of course, it's okay." Dee waved her hand, dismissing his statement as not needing a response from Laney. "You can ride with us, right, Mom?"

"I suppose so." She reluctantly nodded. "The invitation is for anytime after one. We'll probably leave at two."

"Guess I'd better make a quick run to the mall and pick up a pair of swim trunks," Bryce said. He took a step closer to Laney, leaned over and gave her a quick peck on the cheek before she had time to react. "Thanks again for your help today. See you tomorrow, ladies."

As he exited through the gate leading to the front yard, Dee turned to Laney and mouthed, "Oh, my God!"

She motioned frantically toward the house. When they were inside with the door shut tight, she burst out with a verbal, "Oh, my God! He is *so* hot! Vic will just die when she sees him tomorrow!"

"He is a nice-looking man," Laney said.

"Nice-looking? He is absolutely the sexiest man I've ever seen! You must be getting old, Mom, if all you can say is he's nice-looking!"

Oh, if you only knew, Laney thought.

"Well, you and Vicki both need to remember that he's too old for you."

"Old? He can't be more than thirty."

"That's exactly how old he is, and that's too old for you," Laney said sternly.

"Okay, Mom, I promise—I'll look, but I won't touch." Dee raised her right hand as if swearing in court. "Unless he asks real nice."

"Dee!" Laney said.

Her daughter giggled, and in spite of herself, Laney started laughing.

"It's good to see you, honey," she said and hugged her daughter.

They spent the rest of the evening catching up on what had been going on in both their lives. Laney omitted some of the details of hers.

THE BOY NEXT DOOR

Chapter 5

Laney had thought she and Dee might sleep late and have a late breakfast with some quality mother/daughter time, but Dee had other plans. She was up and out of the house by nine to meet her friends for brunch and shopping. Laney settled for a bowl of granola, a cup of tea, and the Sunday paper.

As the morning wore on, she found herself vacillating between anticipation and dread when she thought of the Millers' party. She couldn't deny she was looking forward to spending time with Bryce in a social setting—and seeing him in a swimsuit wouldn't be all bad either. But Greg would be there. He'd had time to think about what Bryce said to him at Applebee's, and knowing her ex like she did, his embarrassment would have morphed into a slow burn of resentment. Seeing Bryce with both his wife and his daughter would only add fuel to the fire.

Dee was another worry. She was smitten with Bryce and doubtless her friends would be as well. Laney didn't know Bryce well enough to guess how he would receive their attentions. What she had said to Dee was true— he was too old for her. He was more experienced than her daughter, and older, more experienced men often took advantage of impressionable young girls. Dee had said that she and her friends had postponed their road trip for a week, so if she could keep Dee from getting into Bryce trouble for that long, he would likely be home in California by the time she got back.

Laney started getting ready for the party before noon, not even bothering to deny to herself why she was putting so much effort into choosing her most flattering swimsuit out of the three she owned. If Dee hadn't invited Bryce, she would have picked her most unflattering suit in the hopes of dampening Greg's enthusiasm. Instead, she chose one she had bought less than a month ago, a green one-piece tropical floral that brought out the green highlights in her hazel eyes. The bust was bow-shaped, gathered in the middle, which pulled the cups in closer, making her boobs look better than they were. The leg openings were cut high, adding even more length to her already long legs. Guests usually arrived at the party already dressed in swimwear, so she would wear the suit with its matching green cover-up. In case she couldn't escape before the evening festivities, she threw a green crinkle skirt that came in its own bag into a pale orange canvas beach bag, along with a spaghetti strap white camisole with a built-in bra.

That done, she turned her attentions on her body. She spent twenty minutes shaving her armpits, legs, and pubic area—Greta called it bush-hogging —until her skin felt completely free of bristles. She spent another ten minutes using an emery board on her nails. Thankfully, she'd gotten a pedicure earlier in the week so her feet were ready to party. She had finished showering and drying her hair and was putting the finishing touches on a little light make-up when she heard the front door slam.

"I'm back," she heard her daughter call above the rustle of bags.

Laney had left her bedroom door open, and Dee appeared there a moment later.

"I found an awesome suit!" Dee said. She opened one of her three bags and pulled out the tiniest bikini Laney had ever seen. The bandeau top sported horizontal red and white stripes and a tie that went from the middle around the back of the neck. The bottom was solid red and barely more than a thong.

"It doesn't look like it covers much," Laney said. She wanted to put her foot down and forbid Dee from wearing it in public, but she stopped herself. Dee was legally an adult and could wear whatever she wanted even if her mother didn't like it.

"Oh, Mom," Dee said in that tone all mothers of daughters hear at one time or another. "I can use my white terry cover-up with it. And I got some shorts and a top for later—and new sandals."

She held up the other two bags.

"It's nearly one," Laney said, glancing at the clock on her nightstand. "You better get ready."

After Dee left to get ready, Laney dressed in her new swimsuit, examined herself from every angle before pulling on the cover-up and tying it at the waist. She slipped gold posts in her ear lobes and low-heeled wedge sandals that strapped around her ankles on her feet. She was ready—or at least as ready as she would ever be. Going to this party was a mistake and there were bound to be fireworks thanks to Greg, but at least she'd look damn good during the fireworks!

Laney heard Dee's shower shut off. It wouldn't take her daughter long now, but there should be enough time to go next door and have a word with Bryce.

He answered the door on her first knock. He was dressed in jeans, a short-sleeved navy-and-white striped tee, and sandals. His eyes turned warm when he saw her, his mouth curling up to one side in that adorable grin. Laney started to return the smile, but stopped herself. She was here to have a serious heart-to-heart with him. Smiling at each other was not part of the plan.

"Hey," he said. "You look great. We ready to leave?"

"Almost," she said. "Dee just got out of the shower. I wanted to talk to you alone."

"I love to talk to you alone, but from the sound of it, I'm not sure I'll like this conversation." He grinned.

"I want you to behave yourself," Laney said, trying to sound stern. "No innuendos, no joking, no comments about me giving you a bath when you were little. Okay?"

He raised his hands in mock surrender. "Whatever you say, love of my life."

"This is a mistake," Laney muttered, turning to go.

Bryce quickly grabbed her arm. "Sorry. I couldn't resist. I promise I won't do anything to embarrass you in front of your daughter."

She looked at him for a moment without speaking. The grin had faded and he looked serious. She wasn't sure she could trust him to remember his promise after he'd had a couple of beers, but what choice did she have? She couldn't avoid going to the party now, and thanks to Dee, she was going to have to take him along.

"I'm trusting you to respect my wishes," she said.

He nodded and let go of her arm. "No problem."

"Greg will be there, too," she said. "I'd appreciate it if you'd do your best to avoid any run-ins with him. After the other day, he'll be ready."

"Best behavior. I promise." He raised his right hand, as if swearing in court. "So—anything I should be taking to this shindig?"

She glanced down at his jeans, trying not to notice the interesting bulge in the center.

"Most people show up in their swimsuits and trunks," she said. "And take a change of clothes if they're planning on staying all day."

"Got my trunks on underneath these." He gestured to his jeans. "I've got a towel, sunscreen, and underwear in my backpack, so I guess I'm good to go. How about I drive?"

"That's not necessary," Laney started. At that moment, Dee came out of the house, both hers and Laney's beach bags over her shoulder.

"Time to party!" she called.

"I'm driving," Bryce called back before Laney could object. "Let me grab my bag."

"Did you lock up?" Laney asked.

"Yep." Dee handed her the house keys.

Bryce returned with his bag and locked his own door.

"We're taking my car," he said.

"Cool," Dee said, and Laney gave up.

Bryce unlocked the rental with the remote and escorted the women to the passenger side. With his hand resting lightly in the small of her back, he directed Laney to the front seat. Dee hopped in the back.

It was a little before two when they pulled up in front of the Millers' large two-story-plus-attic white Colonial. The drive and the street for nearly a block in either direction were packed with cars. Bryce found a spot half a block past their destination and expertly parallel-parked in the tight space.

"The Millers must throw one hell of a shindig," he said.

"The social event of the season," Dee said in a fake snobbish tone.

Bryce laughed and opened his door. Laney quickly opened hers and got out before he had a chance to come around to her side. He locked the car with the remote and the three of them walked back toward the Millers. Laney felt his hand touch her back. She glared at him, and he dropped it to his side. Thankfully Dee hadn't noticed the silent exchange.

Laney, Dee, and Bryce walked around the side of the house and into a back yard completely enclosed by a high wrought iron fence. The Millers' house sat on an acre lot that extended back to a line of flowering shrubs planted to soften the wall separating the property from the service road that bordered the gated community. A table of finger foods and bowls of chips, pretzels, and nuts, along with a bar and beer keg occupied one side of the spacious flagstone patio that connected the house to the enormous kidney-shaped pool and in-ground hot tub. A DJ's platform—empty for now—sat at the far side of the patio. Tables circled the edge of the patio, but the space between the DJ's platform and the caterers had been left empty to accommodate anyone who wanted to dance when the music started playing.

The flagstone continued around the pool where more tables sat, along with chaise lounges and patio chairs.

Laney spotted a few people she knew in the pool and even more lounging poolside or gathered in groups around the beer keg and food table. A volleyball net had been set up on the grass at the back of the spacious yard and teams of teenagers and a few twenty-somethings were battling it out. After a child had nearly drowned in the pool during the early years of their parties, the Millers had specified adults and teens only on the invitations.

"Laney! Dee! Welcome."

Laney turned to see Joanna Miller exiting the house, a drink in one hand. Only a couple of years older than Laney, Joanna looked much older, probably thanks to the tanning beds she visited every day. Her skin was dark and almost leathery. Today it looked even darker in contrast with her white one-piece swimsuit. Her short dark hair was still damp from a dip in the pool. Her eyes took on a predatory glint when she saw Bryce.

"And you brought a guest. How nice!"

"Bryce Adams," Bryce said, extending his hand.

"My pleasure." Joanna nearly purred as she shook Bryce's hand.

Joanna looked like she was about to have an orgasm, and several women in nearby groups were appraising him from head to toe, their heads together. No doubt they were whispering about what they would like to do to him. It looked as if it was shaping up to be a day of women salivating over Bryce. Laney fought the urge to stake her claim by putting her hand on his back. She did not have a claim on him nor, she told herself, did she want one.

"Bryce is the Davidsons' grandson," Laney said. "He's in from California to get their house ready for market."

"Oh, darn," Joanna said, reaching out and touching his shoulder playfully. "I was hoping you had moved to town to stay."

Someone shouted Dee's name from the direction of the pool, and she waved in response.

"There's Vic and Jana." Dee pulled her beach towel from her bag and handed the bag to Laney. "Can you stash this inside for me, Mom?"

Laney nodded. Dee ran off to her friends, both of whom were whispering excitedly while ogling Bryce.

"Hey, Laney," Bill Miller said, coming up behind his wife and draping his arm possessively across her shoulders. "Glad you could make it."

"You know I never miss your party," Laney said, trying to sound more upbeat than she felt.

She introduced Bill and Bryce, repeating the explanation of who Bryce was and what he was doing in town. The two men shook. Bryce was open and friendly, his attention focused on Bill, and Laney saw their host visibly relax his territorial posture. Bryce seemed to know how to put men at ease, even when their women were lusting after him. Probably something he had to learn early, Laney thought, just to keep from getting beat up by insecure husbands.

"Oops, there's the mayor and his wife," Bill said, as a gray-haired couple entered the yard. "Laney, you know where to put your bags. Show Bryce around and we'll talk to you both later."

"Come on," Laney said. "We'll get rid of these bags and I'll show you where the bathrooms are."

She led Bryce through the patio doors into the Millers' stainless steel and granite kitchen. She wondered how much cooking was ever done here. Bill and Joanna were busy corporate lawyers, one or the other usually out-of-town on business. Greta had told her she'd heard they'd recently hired a personal chef to prepare meals in advance, so maybe the microwave got a regular workout even if the rest of the high-end appliances didn't.

Laney pointed to a door leading to a short hall off the left side of the kitchen.

"That leads to the laundry room, half-bath, and garage. The first door on the right is the half-bath." She pointed straight ahead to a pair of swinging doors. "The dining room is through there."

She led Bryce to an opening without a door in the far right corner of the kitchen. It led into a hall that branched out into another hall leading toward the side of the house and another that led to the front. Twenty feet ahead, the section leading to the front widened into a foyer with stairs leading to the second floor.

"The living room is down there to the left," Laney said, gesturing toward the foyer. "Bill's office and most of the bedrooms are upstairs, but Joanna's office and two guest rooms are this way."

She led him down the hall leading toward the side of the house, pointing out a full bath behind the first door on the right. She stopped at the first door on the left ten feet past the bathroom.

"People leave their things in this room," she said, stepping into the bedroom. "But use the bathroom to change clothes or someone might walk in on you."

Bryce wedged his bag among the others on the bed before stripping off his tee. It was the first time she'd seen him shirtless since he'd opened the door to her knock three days ago. His chest looked just as good as she remembered it.

"Bryce, I told you to use the bathroom to change," she said, trying to sound stern.

"I've got my swim trunks on under here, remember?" He unsnapped his jeans and began pulling the zipper down, his eyes never leaving hers, that lopsided grin on his face. "You don't have to watch if you don't want to."

Laney turned away, knowing she was blushing, and tried to look busy finding a place for hers and Dee's bags. When she turned back, he was just straightening up after slipping his jeans over his feet. His legs were tan and sculpted, just as she had imagined them after seeing a hint of their shape through his clothes. His swim trunks were navy and white. She had half expected he'd be wearing bikini trunks to show off his physique, but his were just plain old boxer style, something he'd probably picked up at the local Walmart after Dee had invited him to the party. Of course, bikini trunks were hardly necessary to make his body look good.

Her eyes continued up, lingering for a moment on the bulge just visible in his loose trunks, then over his hard six-pack abdomen, his sculpted chest and broad shoulders—suddenly she realized she was staring and jerked her gaze up to his face. He was looking back, but instead of the amusement she expected to see, his eyes were full of hunger.

"We really should do something about this," he said, his voice low.

Dropping his jeans in a heap on the floor, he took a step forward, reached out and tugged on her cover-up's tie. His gaze drifted slowly over her body. Laney knew someone might walk in at any moment, but she couldn't move, the rush of warmth spreading out from her middle and turning her legs to mush.

"God, you're beautiful," he whispered.

His hand snaked around her waist and he started to pull her to him when they heard a door slam and the sound of people laughing. Laney shook her head and stepped back quickly, retying her cover-up. She stepped through the bedroom door just as Bill and another man came down the hall.

"Hey, Laney, just the woman I was looking for," Bill said. "I want to introduce you to an old college buddy of mine. Rex, this is Laney Mitchell. Laney, Rex Taylor."

Laney guessed the handsome man with Bill was in his late forties, maybe early fifties. He had black hair liberally streaked with gray and the bluest eyes Laney thought she'd ever seen. He was tall and well built, dressed in blue trunks that matched the color of his eyes, a small gym bag hung over one shoulder. His features were strong and his smile warm as he shook her hand.

"Nice to meet you, Laney," he said. He held her hand a moment longer than necessary before releasing it.

"You, too," she managed to say. She heard Bryce step out of the room behind her. Hunks in the back, hunks in the front, here I am stuck in the middle, she thought, and felt an urge to giggle. Bill introduced his friend to Bryce. They exchanged a few pleasantries before Bill and Rex moved on into the guest room.

"Don't forget," Bryce whispered into her ear as they walked down the hall, his warm breath and the touch of his hand on her back causing goose bumps to break out on her arms. "You should always leave with the guy who brought you."

He was grinning that cocky lopsided grin again. One part of her wanted to smack it off his face, but another part—a part that was growing stronger, she realized in dismay—wanted to kiss it off. Appalled at herself, Laney shook off his hand and picked up her pace, hurrying to the safety of a crowd.

Joanna must have been watching for her to come out of the house. As soon as she saw Laney, she hurried over and took her arm.

"Bryce, can I borrow Laney for a moment? Girl talk, you know."

At that moment, Dee called Bryce's name. She and her friends were in the pool, holding onto the side. She waved Bryce over.

"Sure," Bryce said. "You can borrow her. Just be sure to give her back."

Bryce headed over to Dee and her friends and jumped into the pool, splashing the girls' faces and hair in the process. The girls squealed in protest, but it was obvious they were thrilled. They surrounded Bryce and began trying to push him under.

"He is a *doll*!" Joanna said. "I wouldn't want him around my daughter, though—if I had one, that is. I'd rather keep him for myself. Besides, a man like that is bound to break a young girl's heart."

"Dee knows he's too old for her," Laney said.

"Oh, come on!" Joanna raised her eyebrows. "Since when did a little thing like that ever stop a woman? But that's not what I wanted to talk to you about."

She looked over her shoulder at the patio door and guided Laney to the empty DJ platform.

"Did Bill introduce you to his friend, Rex?"

"Yes, he did." Laney nodded. "He seemed like a nice man."

"And not too hard on the eyes either, right?" Joanna winked. "I knew him when Bill and I were in college, and I swear he's improved with age. He used to be a little on the skinny side, but now—all those muscles—anyway, that isn't what I wanted to talk to you about either. Rex is in the area on business, but he won't say what. What we do know is that he's a partner in a company that owns a lot of different businesses. We think he might be your mysterious buyer."

Greg had discussed the sale with Bill over lunch soon after the attorneys representing the buyer had approached them with the offer. Greg hadn't liked not having the buyer's name, but Bill had assured him that it wasn't uncommon for an investment group to use attorneys as intermediaries until everything had checked out and the papers were ready to be signed. A buyer wanted to avoid the complications that could arise if the seller discovered they had deep pockets or that they were strongly motivated to move into an area, fearing that the seller might try to negotiate a higher price.

"If it is Bill's friend," Laney said. "Why would he be here now? We're probably two weeks or more away from signing papers. The buyer might have completed due diligence on the other two clubs, but I haven't gotten Rosedale's books and contracts to them yet."

"Rex told Bill that he was here to try to speed things up on a deal. Have you gotten any requests like that from the attorneys?"

"Not that I've heard."

"Here they come." Joanna nudged Laney. "I'll let you know if we find out anything else."

She moved back from Laney and smiled at her approaching husband and Rex Taylor.

"There you two are," she said. "Honey, can you help me get those folding chairs out of the basement? It looks like we're going to need them."

Rex turned to Laney as Bill and Joanna headed toward the house.

"Nice party," he said.

"Bill and Joanna are great hosts," Laney said. "So you and Bill have been friends since college? Are you from around here?"

He shook his head. "I'm from Michigan, but I've lived in Atlanta for the last twenty years."

"That explains why I haven't seen you at one of these parties before."

"Bill's invited me to come up before," Rex said. "Unfortunately, I was always busy. Had I known there would be beautiful women like you attending, I would have rearranged my schedule."

Laney laughed.

"Oh, you're a smooth talker, aren't you! You and Bill must have been something in college!"

"We were perfect angels—only there to get a good education."

"I bet. I won't ask an education in what!"

Three young men who had been eating at a nearby table got up, tossed their paper plates and plasticware in the trash and headed for the pool.

"Let's grab that." Rex gestured at the table.

He pulled a chair out for her. As she sat down, her gaze drifted to the pool. Bryce, Dee, and her two friends were resting against the side, talking. The three girls were hanging on every word that came out of his mouth, and he seemed to be enjoying the attention. He hadn't been looking her way, but he must have sensed she was looking at him. Their eyes met, then his flicked up at Rex who was just sitting down in the chair to her left. Dee's friend, Vicki, said something to Bryce, but he didn't respond. She tapped him on the shoulder. He looked surprised and turned his attention back to the girls.

"Bill tells me you're divorced," Rex said. "In case you want to know, so am I."

Laney laughed. "You don't beat around the bush, do you?"

"Seize the day, I always say. You have kids?"

"One. A daughter. That's her over there." Laney gestured toward the girls and Bryce. "The blonde in the way-too-skimpy bathing suit."

"Cute girl. Is Mr. Adams her boyfriend?"

"No, of course not! She's only twenty. They just met yesterday."

"Is he your boyfriend?"

"Of course not!" Laney said again. She could feel herself blushing. "Why would you think that?"

"The way he was looking at your butt when he stepped out of the bedroom back there," Rex said. He smiled. "Pretty much the same way I was looking at it when you walked on down the hall."

Holy crap, Laney thought. This is turning into some party! Before she could think of a reply, she saw Greta step into the yard, running late as usual. Relieved, she waved her hand to catch Greta's eye and motioned her over.

"Hey, there." Greta dropped her bag on the patio, cinched the belt of her white terrycloth cover-up tighter, and flopped into the chair across from Laney. "Sorry I'm late."

"Nothing I didn't expect," Laney said.

"You know me too well. Hi, handsome, I'm Greta Crawford." Greta extended her hand.

Rex laughed and shook it. "Rex Taylor. Good to meet you."

"Rex is a college friend of Bill's," Laney said. "He's from Atlanta."

"You drove all the way from Atlanta for this party?" Greta said.

"Not exactly," Rex said. "I was in the area on business anyway, so when Bill invited me, I accepted. I'm very glad I did now that I've met two such charming ladies."

"I like this guy," Greta stage-whispered to Laney and Rex laughed. Greta stood. "I need a drink. Either of you want anything?"

"I'll take a beer. Any kind." Rex said. "Laney?"

"Grab me a wine cooler." Laney usually waited until the DJ started playing to have a drink, but between Bryce and Rex, she felt the need for one. She was getting flustered with all the attention and flirting.

Maybe a little false courage compliments of alcohol would help.

Laney watched as Greta ordered two wine coolers and a beer from a young man at the caterer's table and helped herself to some finger food while she waited for the drinks. She was almost to the table when she looked up in surprise.

"Hey, Bryce," Greta said. "I didn't expect to see you here."

Laney looked up to see Bryce approaching the table, water droplets trickling over his chest. His towel was draped around his shoulders, his hair tousled from the drying he'd given it.

"Hi, Greta. Dee and Laney were nice enough to invite me yesterday." He winked at Laney. "Nothing I like better than escorting two beautiful women to parties."

He sat down in the chair on Laney's right and nodded at Rex. Rex nodded back. Greta looked at Laney, her eyes wide.

"So are you from around here, Rex?" Bryce said.

"Just in town on business. I'm from Atlanta. How about you?"

"I'm from California, but I used to live here."

"Bryce's grandmother owns the house next door to mine," Laney said, ignoring Greta's amused expression as she looked from one man to the other, then at Laney. "She lives in California now, too. He's here getting the house ready to put on the market."

"I lived next to this lady when I was a kid," Bryce said, squeezing Laney's shoulder. "Would you believe she was my babysitter?"

Rex laughed in surprise. "Babysitter? No kidding."

"No kidding," Laney said.

"How old were you?" Rex asked Bryce.

"I was four, wasn't I, when you first started sitting me?" Bryce said. "I was five when we moved to California."

"You had just had your fourth birthday a couple of weeks before the first time I watched you," Laney said, smiling at the memory of the cute little boy who had shyly asked if she wanted to play with the dinosaurs he'd gotten for his birthday.

"And how old were you?" Rex turned to Laney.

"He's trying to find out your age," Greta said. She punched Rex on the arm. "You really think my friend is dumb enough to fall for that?"

"Ignore her," Laney said. "I was fifteen."

"So you two have known each other a long time," Rex said, looking from Laney to Bryce.

"Not really," Laney said. "Until last Thursday, I hadn't seen Bryce since he moved to California."

"And we're making up for lost time, aren't we?" Bryce winked at Laney.

Before she could think of a reply, she heard Dee yell, "Hey, Dad!"

Oh, this just keeps getting better, Laney thought.

Dee climbed out of the pool and met her dad when he was halfway to the patio. She threw her arms around him and hugged him. Laney saw Greg flinch as she pressed her pool-soaked body against him, then he hugged her back. Then he pushed her an arm's length away and eyed her swimsuit disapprovingly. He said something to her that Laney couldn't hear, but she knew he was telling her she was exposing too much skin. You're wasting your breath, Laney thought, but thanks for trying anyway.

Dee took after her father in looks. She had his blond hair, his green eyes, and his fair complexion. Even their facial features were similar, allowing for the difference in gender. Laney felt a pang of sadness that she could see nothing of herself in her daughter.

Dee took Greg's hand and led him over to the table. She gestured to Bryce.

"Dad, this is Bryce Adams. His grandparents own the house next door to Mom. Would you believe it—she was his babysitter when she was in high school!"

"I've heard all about it," Greg said. "Hello, Laney, Greta. Bryce."

"You have?" Dee looked puzzled. "When?"

"We met Friday at Applebee's," Greg said.

"Oh," Dee said.

Greta directed a look at Laney that said, "What else are you not telling me?"

Laney ignored her.

Greg turned to Rex and extended his hand. "Greg Mitchell."

"Rex Taylor." Rex stood and the two men shook. "I gather you're Laney's ex."

"My claim to fame," Greg said. His lips were smiling, but the smile didn't reach his eyes. "Laney, can I talk to you a minute? In private?"

Bryce leaned forward in his chair, hands resting on the arms as if about to stand, and Rex moved his feet into a wider stance. Good God, Laney thought. In another minute, they'll be peeing to mark territory! I wish I'd stayed home! Greta was having a great time watching the drama, her eyes moving from one man to the other, her eyes wide, her wine cooler forgotten. Laney could just imagine what she would say when she got the chance.

"Of course," Laney said and stood. "Excuse me for a moment."

Greg led the way through the patio door into the kitchen. The sound of voices down the hall toward the bedroom indicated they weren't alone in the house, so he continued on into the entrance hall, then out the front door onto the covered porch that stretched across the front of the house. As she shut the door behind her, he turned to her. He looked so angry, a cartoonist would have portrayed him with steam coming out of his ears.

"What the hell are you doing bringing your 'boy toy' here with our daughter and all of our friends?"

Laney's mouth dropped open. "How dare you! Not that you have any right to know, but there is nothing going on between Bryce and me."

"That's not what it sounded like at Applebee's."

"He was yanking your chain, Greg."

"And why would he want to do that?" Greg demanded. "I suppose you've been crying on his shoulder about how awful I treated you. I know I made a mistake, but I've apologized. You just can't let it go, can you?"

"A mistake?" Laney realized she was clenching her fists and forced herself to open them. "Is that what you call screwing around on your wife? A mistake? I caught you in one 'mistake,' but I've found out since that there were plenty of others."

"I don't know what you're talking about," Greg started, but Laney interrupted.

"Don't even bother, Greg," she said, her anger suddenly gone. "It doesn't matter anymore. What does matter, though, is that I'm sick of you hounding me. We are *not* getting back together. You are now single and so am I. And that means if I want to have a 'boy toy' or any other kind of relationship, I will."

"Just to embarrass me, right?"

Laney threw up her hands in disgust and turned back to the front door. "I give up."

"So if you're not banging the kid from next door, maybe it's that old stud. Is that it?"

Laney turned back to him, confused for a second. Then she realized he was talking about Rex.

"Are you talking about the other man at the table with Greta and me?"

Greg nodded. "So who is he?"

"Again, not that you have any right to know, I just met him today. He's a college friend of Bill's. And he doesn't look old to me, although . . . ," she just couldn't resist, "I'll admit he does look like a stud."

Greg looked like she'd slapped him. Oh, you are so easy, she thought. Then she remembered what Joanna had told her. Even though she badly wanted to let Greg continue to worry about what Rex and she might be up to, there was the sale of Bodies to consider. It would be just her luck for Greg to go back to the party and start something with Rex.

"For your information," she said, "Joanna told me that Rex is a partner in a group that buys up businesses. He's in town to close a deal, but hasn't told them any details. She and Bill think he might be our buyer."

All concern about whether she was sleeping with Rex seemed to vanish instantly from Greg's mind, and he was all business.

"Is that right?" he said.

"That's what they think. Of course, they could be wrong and he's here for another reason."

"He hasn't said anything to you?"

"Oh, he's said plenty, but nothing about what his business is." Laney could see the innuendo had slipped past him. "Joanna said he told them he was in town to try to speed up a closing. Have the attorneys contacted you about anything like that?"

Greg shook his head.

"So maybe he's not our buyer," Laney said. "I'm sure we're not the only business in town that's selling."

"Maybe he'll let something slip to you."

"Oh, so now you want me to go undercover with the old stud," she said. "That might not be so bad."

"Oh, come on, Laney," Greg said in the tone he had used too often during their marriage, a tone that he would use to placate a pouting child. She fought the urge to smack him. "You know how I get where you're concerned. You know I still love you. The thought of you with someone else . . . it makes me crazy."

He reached out and took her by the arm.

"Come here," he said. "Let's kiss and make up."

Laney yanked her arm out of his grasp. "Not in your wildest dreams, Greg."

She crossed to the front door, but stopped with her hand on the doorknob, turning back to him.

"You've got to stop this, Greg," she said. "I am not coming back to you. We're done. I admit you hurt me, but I forgive you. I've moved on, and you need to as well. For Dee's sake, if nothing else."

He started to reply, but she opened the door, stepped inside, and closed it before he could. She stopped in the half bath off the hall to the laundry room to gain time to compose herself. Greg irritated like a burr under a saddle, but because Dee was in their world, there was no way she could ever rid herself of him completely. She used the toilet, flushed, and examined herself in the mirror. She was a little flushed, but that could be attributed to being in the sun.

Back outside, her three tablemates looked at her inquiringly.

"Everything okay?" Bryce asked.

"Hunky dory," she replied. "But I think it's time to cool off with a swim."

Chapter 6

Greg stayed on his best behavior throughout the rest of the afternoon. He avoided Laney's table, although she caught him looking her way more than once. He joined Dee and her friends on a volleyball team, swam, and mingled with friends around the pool. Once he approached Rex at the beer keg and they had a short, but apparently civil, conversation. Laney knew she didn't have to worry about him making a scene with Rex now that he thought Rex might be their buyer. No matter how jealous he might be of Rex's attention to her, Greg would never do anything that might jeopardize the sale. He avoided Bryce completely, and thankfully Bryce did the same. Dee had tried to get him to play on the same volleyball game as Greg, but Bryce managed to come up with excuses why he couldn't play. When Dee moved away from the table, Laney smiled her thanks at Bryce.

As day moved into evening, the caterers fired up two large gas grills and began cooking burgers, ribs, and chicken strips. The finger foods were replaced by bowls of beans, slaw, and potato, pasta, and bean salads, along with wicked-looking desserts and bowls of fresh fruit for people who could resist the temptation of the calorie-laden sweets. The pool emptied and the volleyball games stopped as guests filled paper plates with food. Laney waited until several people had gotten into line behind Greg before she stood up to go to the grill. The others had waited for her cue and the four of them went up together.

As they ate, Laney decided that she was glad she came after all. It had been a perfect June day weather-wise and the evening promised to be even better. The sky was clear and the air was warm, but not muggy—just the right temperature for an outdoor party. Bryce and Rex had both been on their best behavior, friendly to one another and casual with her. Greta looked a little disappointed there hadn't been any more drama, but that was Greta. Dee was having a blast, and Greg was being good after his initial tantrum. Good food, great weather, family, friends, and a couple of really sexy guys sitting at your table making you the envy of every woman at the party—well, there could be worse ways to spend a Sunday afternoon!

As the food disappeared, the younger people returned to the pool and volleyball, while the adults drifted into the house in swimwear and out in street clothes. Laney and Greta shared the hall bath while changing.

"So which one's it gonna be?" Greta asked as soon as the door was locked behind them.

"Which one what?" Laney said, although she had a pretty good idea of Greta's meaning.

"Bryce or Rex? Which one are you going to get it on with? Or maybe I should say, which one are you going to get it on with first?"

"Greta!" Laney was a little shocked.

"Oh, come on, I was only kidding about the 'which one first' thing," Greta said. "I know you wouldn't do that. Now, if I were single . . . ah, but those kind of thoughts are best reserved for the nights when Lee isn't home and my vibrator is."

Laney tried to hide her smile. Greta had fantasies of sluttiness, but that's all they were—fantasies. She and Lee were devoted to one another, and according to Greta, their sex life was as active as the day they were married thanks to the frequent separations required by Lee's job.

"And, by the way, I didn't think you were going to invite Bryce to this party."

"I didn't. Dee did. She showed up yesterday evening while we were cooking out and invited him before I had a chance to say anything to her."

"Cooking out? Why are you keeping all these secrets from me? When I saw you yesterday morning, you were going to help him pick out carpet and paint, and that was that."

"We did that—or tried. He couldn't make up his mind. Afterwards we went for a drive around town and out in the country, and the next thing I knew we were grilling out." Laney shrugged her shoulders. "What can I say? He's very persuasive."

Greta laughed. "I bet. And I bet he'll persuade himself right into your pants."

"No, he will not," Laney said. "I do not intend to sleep with a man I used to babysit."

"Umm-hmmm. Methinks the lady doth protest too much."

"I give up," Laney muttered.

"But," Greta continued. "If by some miracle you resist Bryce's charms, Mr. Rex Taylor wouldn't be a bad second choice. That is, unless he's too old for you."

"Sarcasm does not become you," Laney said.

"You and Greg have been history for, what, three years now, and you haven't been on a date, much less gotten laid. Unless you're keeping secrets from me and that's pretty hard to do. You've come up with reasons to turn down every man who's asked you."

"I've been busy, that's all."

"Bull! You're afraid, that's all. And after Greg, I can understand that, but life goes on, sweetie. Before you know it, you'll be all saggy and wrinkled, and you'll wish you had taken some of those guys up on their offers."

"Boy, aren't you a ray of sunshine!"

"Just telling it like it is. Relax for a change and have some fun. I can think of two guys who are more than willing to help you in that department. Personally, I'd choose the young stud over the old one, but I wouldn't kick either one of them out of bed for eating crackers."

Laney shook her head and burst out laughing. A second later, Greta joined her. They were still cracking up as they exited the bathroom, getting a few strange looks from three teens talking in the kitchen.

The DJ had arrived and was setting up his equipment. It was a few minutes past eight-thirty, and the light was starting to soften as the sun slipped toward the horizon. Rex had dressed in white slacks and a blue short-sleeved tee that matched his eyes. Laney wondered if he consciously chose his clothing to complement them, and couldn't stop herself from remembering that Greg preferred certain shades of green for his shirts because they brought out the color of his eyes. It had always seemed narcissistic to her, but it was unfair to think that way. Women did that sort of thing all the time—she often did it herself—so why shouldn't men? Just because they took steps to look their best didn't mean they couldn't love someone else as much as they loved themselves.

Bryce was dressed in the jeans and tee he had arrived in. She doubted Bryce gave much thought to whether his clothes flattered the color of his eyes or anything else, but then he didn't have to. He could wear a cardboard box and it would look good. Still, both Greg and Rex were handsome men, so why did they spend more time on themselves? Maybe it was something that came with age, and one day Bryce would be getting manicures and choosing his clothing based on whether the color emphasized his eyes.

The men were talking golf over draft beers, but stopped as she and Greta walked up to the table.

"Looks like we're ready for the evening festivities," Rex said. "Anyone ready for another drink?"

Laney decided another wine cooler wouldn't hurt. She and Greta gave their orders, and the men jumped up to fill them.

"So which one are you going to dance with first?"

"Will you stop?"

"Hey, I said 'dance,' not 'sleep with.' Give me some credit for trying to clean up my act."

The DJ started off slow with *Endless Love*. Bryce reached the table before Rex, his eyes on Laney. He set the drinks he was carrying on the table, and just as he opened his mouth—to ask her to dance, she knew—Dee grabbed his hand.

"Let's dance," she said, pulling him toward the dance floor. He hesitated for a second, looking at Laney, then followed Dee.

"Care to dance?" Rex asked.

She nodded, wondering how Greta would score this one. If Dee hadn't interfered, Bryce would have been the first. For a second, she wished her daughter had gone on her road trip and missed the party, then chided herself both for being a bad mother and for that little pang of jealousy she felt. She had to remember that Bryce was not good for either of them.

Rex was a good dancer. He held her close, his breath warm on her neck, making her very aware of his body. She was also aware of Greg watching them from a poolside table. It was obvious he didn't like what he was seeing, but Laney knew he would behave himself now that he thought Rex might be their buyer. She noticed Greg's gaze occasionally move from them to someone else on the dance floor, and knew he was watching Bryce with Dee. Based on the hardening of his expression, he liked that even less than he liked seeing her with Rex.

As she and Rex moved and turned with the music, she saw that Bryce was being careful to keep a respectable distance between himself and her daughter, while Dee was doing her best to close the gap. Dee would move into Bryce, once resting her face on his shoulder, and with the next step, he would casually move back an inch or two. There wasn't much doubt that her daughter was sending signals, but Bryce was doing his best to block them. That was probably the only reason Greg hadn't already stomped onto the floor and made a scene.

The slow song ended and was replaced by a fast one. As Rex and Laney left the dance floor, she noticed that Dee had hung on to Bryce for a fast dance. He looked like he knew what he was doing on the dance floor, but he didn't look happy about doing it. Was she imagining it or did he keep glancing her way?

"What's the matter?" Greta said as they reached the table. "You old folks can't keep up with the kids?"

"Of course, we can," Rex said, pulling Laney's chair out for her. "But slow dances are much more fun."

"I hear that," Greta said.

Dee tried to keep Bryce on the dance floor after the song ended, but he begged off. Dee accompanied him to the table and pulled out her cell phone.

"We need to get some pictures before the sun is completely gone," she said, holding the phone up and clicking a shot of Greta, Rex, and Laney seated at the table. She slid one arm around Bryce's waist and held the camera out at arm's length.

"Best selfie ever," she said, snapping the picture. She slipped it back into her pocket. "Give me your phone. You need some pics, too."

Bryce pulled his phone from his pants pocket and gave it to her. Dee took another selfie of the two of them with his phone. Laney thought he had a funny look on his face, a look that said he was feeling trapped. Or was that just wishful thinking on her part? And if it was wishful thinking, was she glad he wasn't encouraging her daughter's advances for her daughter's sake or for her own? Was she really allowing herself to get in the position of competing with her daughter for a man, even if the competition was just a fantasy she never intended to act on?

Bryce pulled away after Dee was done and sat down. Dee took a couple of shots from different angles of the four of them at the table, then turned and took a few shots of the dance floor and the pool. A phone rang and Laney recognized the sound of her daughter's ringtone. Dee fished the phone out of the pocket of her cover-up and said hello, while handing Bryce his phone. She gave them a one-fingered wave and moved back toward her friends by the pool.

"Let's slow it down again," the DJ announced over the mic. "Grab your lady, guys, and tell her to do it to you one more time."

Do That To Me One More Time by Captain and Tennille began playing. Rex started to speak, but before he could get the words out, Bryce took Laney's hand and led her onto the dance floor. She found it hard to breathe as he pulled her close against his chest and felt the bare skin of his arms touch the bare skin of hers. He hadn't asked her to dance, hadn't spoken a word, simply took her into his arms as if claiming her as his own. The thought excited her. Her heart was pounding as hard as if she'd just run a race, and she was tingly and warm in places that hadn't been tingly and warm in a long time.

As they began to move to the music, she rested her head against his shoulder, her face pressed against his neck. She inhaled deeply, breathing in his smell, a mix of shampoo and after-shave and a heady scent that was his own. She exhaled slowly, her breath caressing his neck. A tremor ran through him at the touch of her breath against his skin, and she felt a sense of power that she had been the cause. He kissed the top of her head before resting his cheek against her hair; she closed her eyes, giving herself up to the movement of his body. Her nipples rubbed against his hard chest, growing hard and sensitive as they moved against his warmth. She pressed even closer, reluctant to leave even a millimeter of space between their bodies, and felt the bulge of his penis against her groin as they swayed to the music. It took all the willpower she had to keep herself from grinding against it as she imagined what it would feel like to have it inside her. The song was the perfect soundtrack, Laney thought, finally admitting to herself that she could never get enough of a man like Bryce. The rest of the party disappeared for her, leaving only the two of them in each other's arms. She wanted it to go on forever.

"May I cut in?"

Laney's head jerked upright, her eyes snapping open, pulled rudely back into the world of the party by Greg's voice. He was standing behind Bryce, and he didn't look happy.

"May I cut in?" he repeated, obviously growing angrier at being ignored.

"No," Bryce said, and whirled Laney away, putting three other couples between Greg and themselves.

Greta and Rex were dancing a few feet away. Both of them had their eyes on Greg, who was staring after Bryce and Laney, fists clenched, face flushed. He started toward them. Greta said something to Rex, and they broke apart, Greta heading for Greg. She intercepted him before he'd taken more than three steps and put her arms around him as if to dance. He tried to get around her, but she leaned close and said something in his ear. Laney had a pretty good idea her friend was telling him not to make a scene in front of his daughter and her friends. Greg hesitated, then began dancing with Greta. Rex had been watching the exchange, ready to intervene if necessary, but now he relaxed and returned to their table.

Laney looked around and realized several other couples on the dance floor were watching, their attention drawn by the tone of Greg's voice and his body language. She felt her face redden, angry with Greg for embarrassing her, but also angry with herself for setting the stage. She moved back an inch or two from Bryce. She felt a gentle pull as he tried to draw her back against his body, but she resisted and he let up. She looked up and found him watching her, his eyes tender.

"I'm sorry," he said. "I didn't mean to cause a scene."

"You didn't," she said. At least not by yourself, she thought. I was a willing partner.

The song ended, and they returned to the table. She looked around for Dee and was relieved to find that she and her friends were involved in another volleyball game. Her daughter hadn't seen either her father or her mother acting like fools. What had she been thinking, practically making love with Bryce in public like that? Dee might not have seen it, but plenty of others had, especially after Greg called their attention to it.

Greta hadn't yet returned to the table. Laney searched the crowd for her and saw her with Greg in the shadows just off the patio. She seemed to be having a heart-to-heart with him. Laney doubted it would do any good in the long term, but hoped it would be enough to keep him in control for the rest of the party.

Rex was watching her, occasionally glancing at Bryce, who was also watching Greta and Greg.

"I'm sorry about all that," Laney said to Rex. "I think Greg's had a little too much to drink."

"He might have," Rex said. "Or maybe he's realizing he lost a good thing."

Bryce glanced at him, smiling slightly before looking back at Greta and Greg. They were walking toward the side gate now, and Greta seemed to have calmed him down. They stepped through the gate and disappeared from view around the side of the house. Bryce looked at Laney, the question evident in his eyes.

"It's okay," she said. "Greta can handle him."

Greta came back through the gate about ten minutes later. She caught Laney's eye and motioned with her head toward the house.

"Be right back," Laney said.

The two met at the door, but didn't speak until they were locked inside the hall bath.

"Sweetie, your life is starting to resemble a soap opera!" Greta's eyes were sparkling. "I mean, two incredibly sexy men trying to get in your pants and an ex-husband ready to duke it out over you! I gotta say, I'm honored to be your friend!"

"Knock it off, Greta," Laney said. "It's not funny."

"No, it's not funny, but it is exciting."

"My daughter is at this party. I don't want 'exciting' around her."

"No, I guess not." Greta turned serious. "I wasn't watching her—did she see what happened?"

"No. At least I don't think so. She and her friends were at the volleyball net and the game looked pretty intense. Where's Greg now?"

"I convinced him to head home."

"Is he safe to drive?"

"He wasn't drunk, Laney. He was fine to drive, although he might be a distracted driver, what with thinking up ways to castrate Bryce. Alcohol's not why he acted like he did."

Greta shook her head.

"If Dee wasn't here, I don't think he would have listened to me, but he didn't want to make a scene in front of her. I also mentioned he didn't need to make a scene in front of Rex either in case he's your buyer, but I guess it's a little late for that. Rex saw it all."

Greta smiled, her eyes lighting up again.

"And he was more than ready to come to your defense out there on the dance floor. Did you switch perfumes or something? Both Bryce and Rex are hot on your scent. And speaking of hot, I about had an orgasm just watching you and Bryce dancing!"

Laney groaned and collapsed against the door.

"I know," she said. "I don't know what got into me."

"I think you just figured out who you want to get into you," Greta said. "That's what happened."

"I can't believe I let myself dance with him like that! Thank God Dee didn't see it."

"Dee is a complication," Greta said. "You know she has the hots for Bryce, don't you?"

"It's been a little hard to miss."

"And did you also see that he did not encourage it? In fact, I'd say he did his best to discourage it without being mean or rude. He wants the momma, not the daughter. And momma wants him, too, don't you?"

Greta stared at her, demanding an answer. Laney sighed.

"Okay, Greta, yes, I want him. I think more than I've ever wanted anybody. But it's just a physical attraction, that's all. He's young, he's sexy, and he seems to be a nice guy. What woman wouldn't want to go to bed with a man like that? What I have to remember is that I'm eleven years older than he is. A hot night of sex is all it could ever be, and is that worth all the risk?"

"Oh, I'd say it would very much be worth it, but that's just me."

Laney pushed away from the door. "I don't agree. I've got Dee to think about. He's too old for her, but it would still be hurtful to her—and embarrassing—to know her mother had a 'boy toy,' as Greg so colorfully put it."

She opened the door, then stopped and turned to Greta.

"Could you do me another favor and check out front to make sure Greg has left? I don't want to run into him on the street when Bryce takes Dee and me home."

Greta nodded and turned toward the front door, while Laney went out the back.

Bryce and Rex looked up as she approached the table, concerned looks on both their faces.

"Everything okay?" Bryce asked.

Laney nodded. "Greta talked Greg into leaving. She's checking now to make sure he actually did."

She sat down and took a sip of her wine cooler.

"I am so sorry about all that," she said, looking from Bryce to Rex and back.

"No need for you to apologize," Rex said. "Your ex is the one who made an ass of himself."

Oh, Lord, Laney thought. If Rex really is our buyer and Greg has messed anything up by his juvenile behavior, I will kill him!

"He doesn't normally act like that. He probably had a little too much to drink. Although," she added, "Greta said he was safe to drive and I trust her judgment."

She hoped she hadn't made things worse. Rex might be just as turned off by a man who drove intoxicated as by one ready to fight over a woman.

"Coast is clear," Greta announced. None of them had seen her approach the table. "Anybody up for another round?"

Laney spent the next hour mingling with other guests at the party and only spending a few minutes at a time at the table. She knew if she didn't avoid Bryce, he'd ask her to dance again and she couldn't let that happen. She'd been lucky the first time that Dee hadn't seen them, but she couldn't expect that luck to hold out forever. Once, while she was talking to some people she knew from Bodies, she saw Bryce start her way. Greta cut him off and pulled him to the dance floor, where she had what appeared to be a serious talk with him while they danced. She hadn't told Greta why she was avoiding the table, but being the good friend that she was, she instinctively knew and was explaining it to Bryce. For a second she worried that her friend might also tell Bryce of her attraction to him, but quickly realized that was a pointless worry for two reasons. First, Greta would never betray her confidence like that, and second, it was unlikely that Bryce needed anyone to tell him.

The crowd began to thin as guests said their goodbyes to their hosts and headed for their cars. The volleyball game had ended. Dee broke away from a cluster of her friends and headed for the table. Time to go home, Laney thought, and made her way back to the table just in time to hear Dee invite Bryce to another party.

"Come on. Don't be such a baby." Dee poked Bryce in the ribs. "It's not *that* late. Trust me, it will be fun."

Bryce raised his hands, palms out. "Can't do it, Dee. Sorry. I have to take your mom home, remember? You guys rode with me."

"Greta can drop her off. Can't you, Greta?"

Bryce shook his head firmly before Greta could respond. "Maybe some other time, Dee. I've got to get up early tomorrow and get some stuff done, or I'll never get this house ready for market."

"Pooh!" Dee stuck her tongue out at him. "You are such a baby! You'll miss a great party."

"I don't doubt it."

"What party?" Laney asked.

"Mark Anderson's invited a bunch of us over to his house." Laney opened her mouth to speak, but Dee waved her hand at her. "I promise I won't drink, Mom. You don't have to worry about me driving drunk."

Laney wanted to protest that her little girl should come home with her now and go straight to bed, but she bit her tongue. Her little girl wasn't little anymore. She might not be of legal drinking age, but she was an adult.

"Okay," she said, even though Dee wasn't asking permission. "Just be careful."

"Yes, Mommy Dearest." Dee kissed her on the cheek and hurried back to her friends.

Rex had been watching the exchange between Dee, Bryce, and Laney, an amused smile on his face.

"So I guess you don't need a ride home, then, right?" he said.

Bryce smiled slightly as Laney shook her head.

"Dee and I rode with Bryce," she said.

Rex stood. "Well, I guess I'll head on out then. It's been great meeting all of you."

He kissed Greta on the cheek before turning to Laney.

"I'd like to see one of your clubs," he said. "Is it possible to get some guest passes?"

"Of course. I'll be at the Rosedale Bodies most mornings this week. Or if you can't make it in the morning, I can leave passes for you at the front desk."

"I'll make it." He kissed her on the cheek, his left hand on her arm. The kiss lasted just a fraction of a second longer than the kiss he'd given Greta. He stepped back and turned to Bryce, extending his hand. "Don't keep this lady up too late, Bryce."

The two men shook. They were both smiling slightly, a look in their eyes that said they both recognized the subtext in Rex's comment. She suddenly realized these two men actually liked one another, and were enjoying the friendly competition they were engaged in. She wasn't sure how she felt about that, knowing she was the "prize" in the competition.

They said their goodbyes to Joanna and Bill. Greta had decided to stay and help the Millers clean up. As she hugged Laney goodbye, she whispered, "Details, remember? I want details!"

Laney ignored her.

As they rounded the front corner of the house, Laney half expected to see Greg waiting, but he'd kept his promise and gone home—or, at least, not come back to the party. That was one worry off her mind, but the other worry was walking next to her.

She was going to be alone in the car with Bryce, it was dark, and they'd spent an evening together that had ratcheted up the sexual tension between them to the point that she couldn't ignore it anymore. Her body was tingling in anticipation of what might happen, but worse, it was tingling in anticipation of what she *wanted* to happen.

They walked to the car in silence, Bryce's hand in its usual place on the small of her back. He unlocked the car with the remote and opened the passenger door for her. She got in without looking at him. He closed it, came around the car, and got into the driver's side. They buckled up, still without speaking, and he started the car.

"You could have gone to the party, you know."

"I don't think a party of underage kids is the place for a thirty-year-old man, do you?" He smiled that adorable crooked smile and reached out to brush her hair back from her face. "Not that that's the main reason I turned it down."

Without meaning to, Laney tilted her head slightly, pressing her cheek against his hand. He leaned toward her, his hand sliding around to the back of her neck. Just as she started to meet him halfway, they heard someone shout to someone else a few cars behind them.

It sounded like one of Dee's friends. Laney quickly sat back in her seat, while Bryce put the car in gear and pulled away from the curb.

Bryce tuned the radio to a blues station and turned the volume low. They didn't speak on the way home, but halfway there, he took her left hand in his right, brought it to his lips, kissed it, then lowered their clasped hands to his hard thigh. Laney made no attempt to pull her hand away, instead savoring the feel of his skin against hers and the muscles flexing in his thigh as he worked the gas pedal.

Her heart sped up as they turned onto her street. She was finding it hard to breathe. Bryce turned into his driveway and pulled along the side of the house, away from the glow cast by the streetlights. He turned off the ignition, let go of her hand and unbuckled his seat belt. Laney undid hers, and as if their movements were choreographed, they moved in tandem, arms sliding around one another, his lips forcing hers open, their tongues entwining. He moved toward the center of the bench seat, turning his body to face her. His hand slid down to her buttocks, pulling her hard against him, and she went willingly. A little voice in her head was screaming that she needed to get a grip, that this was a bad idea, but the little voice was getting harder and harder to hear over her body telling her it was the best idea she'd had in a long time.

"I've wanted to do this since I opened my door and found you standing there," he whispered, as he planted kisses starting from her ear and moving down the side of her neck to the spot where it joined her shoulder. A tremor ran through her body and she groaned.

His right hand was around her waist, holding her firmly against him, while his left hand moved down over her back and cupped her buttocks. He pulled her onto his lap, facing him, her skirt hiked up, her legs on either side of his. As she settled onto his lap, he lifted his lower body and she felt his erection straining against his jeans. She grasped him by the hair and lowered her lips to his, grinding against him like she had wanted to on the dance floor. Time seemed to stop and the outside world disappeared. The feel of this man, the scent and taste of him, the sound of his ragged breathing filled her senses, leaving no room for anything else. She had been right—she would never be able to get enough of him.

"Stay with me tonight," he murmured between kisses. "Stay with me."

An image of his naked body on a sheet flashed into her mind, and she wanted nothing more than to accept his invitation. But on the heels of that delicious image came one of Dee coming home to an empty house and jumping to the obvious conclusion. She pulled back and looked at him. God, he is gorgeous, she thought! His hair lay in a tangled mass of waves around his face, his eyes filled with hunger for her, his lips parted in readiness to claim hers again. At that moment she wanted nothing more than to go inside the Davidsons' house and spend the hours left until dawn making love to him, but this wasn't the time.

"I can't," she said. "I want to—God, I want to—but I can't. When Dee comes home. . . ."

She left the sentence unfinished. He pulled her to him and kissed her, a long, probing kiss that she wanted to go on forever, then released her. He took a deep breath and smiled that crooked little smile she adored.

"When did you say your kid is leaving on her road trip?"

Laney laughed.

"Soon, I hope," she said. She brushed his hair back and kissed his forehead, then slid off his lap and back to her side of the car, his arm still around her waist.

"I second that," he said. He kissed her again. "I'll walk you to your door."

"That's a terrible idea," she said, snuggling against him. "Too much temptation to drag you inside."

He chuckled. "Okay, I'll just watch until you're in. Then I'll go take a very cold shower."

He kissed her once more, a short friendly peck on the cheek, then let her go. They got out of the car, Bryce standing for a moment on his side to adjust his jeans. He turned and saw her watching him across the roof of the car.

"Good thing the light is dim," he said, smiling. "Or I might embarrass myself. Now get inside before I change my mind and drag you into my house."

At the door, she turned. He was standing at the back of his car, watching. She gave him a slight wave and went inside.

As she removed her makeup and brushed her teeth, she replayed everything that had happened that evening. The rational part of her mind still insisted that getting involved with him was a mistake. He was too young for her and he would leave. Could she make love with him—undoubtedly amazing love—then go on with her life when he returned to California and went on with his? She no longer worried that she was just a lark for him, something to brag about to his California buddies. He might be young, but he was very much a man, not a silly boy. But there was no denying that distance in both years and miles would eventually bring an end to anything they might have. She would be taking a big chance on a broken heart.

She lay for a long time, unable to sleep, her body still tingling from his touch, her mind still struggling with the pros and cons. Just before sleep finally claimed her, she knew that she would take the chance.

Chapter 7

The ringing of the phone beside her bed woke her at three in the morning. She came awake instantly, the way she always did when the phone rang in the middle of the night. A phone call at that time was never a harbinger of good news.

"Hello?" She pulled herself to a sitting position, propped against the headboard.

"You tell that son-of-a-bitch Adams to stay away from my daughter!"

"Greg?"

"Of course, it's Greg! You have a daughter with anyone else?"

Laney didn't think she had ever heard Greg so angry. Was he drunk? He must have gone somewhere after leaving the party and continued drinking and brooding on his dislike of Bryce's dancing with Dee. She began to feel more than a little angry herself.

"What do you think you're doing calling me at this hour to bitch about Bryce?" She swung her legs over the side of the bed. "Go to bed, Greg, and sleep it off!"

"I was asleep, dammit!" he said. "Until our daughter came in crying!"

"Dee?" Laney's heart seemed to skip a beat. "What's wrong? What happened? Is she okay?"

"No, she's not okay! She's bawling and throwing up and drunk as hell! Adams got her drunk and who knows what else he did to her!"

"What are you talking about?" Laney was growing more confused by the minute. "I don't understand. I'd better come over."

"No, stay where you are. Dee's too upset to talk about Adams or what happened."

"But it couldn't have been Bryce, Greg. He wasn't with her. She went to a party with some friends. He brought me home and then he went home."

"Well, he didn't stay there," Greg said. "He just dropped her off here, drunk, sick, and crying. I tried to get her to talk about it, but she can't stop crying long enough. If he touched her, I'll kill the son-of-a-bitch!"

"It must have been someone else." Laney slipped her feet into her slippers. "He wasn't with Dee."

"What—so now you're calling your daughter a liar? You can't believe your boy-toy is capable of such a thing?" Greg snorted. "Some mother you are! You tell your 'friend' that I will see him in court over this!"

Laney winced as he slammed the phone down in her ear. She replaced the handset in its cradle, stood, and pulled on her robe. Sleep was out of the question for the time being. Maybe some warm milk would help settle her back down.

It didn't make any sense. Maybe it was someone Dee knew who was also named Bryce and Greg had misunderstood. His dislike of Bryce could easily lead him to jump to the wrong conclusion. At least Dee was safe at her father's house. That was all that mattered. Whatever else had happened, they would get through it together.

She was pouring milk into a cup to heat in the microwave when lights swung across her living room drapes the way headlights always did when a car pulled into the Davidsons' drive. Setting the carton down, she crossed the darkened living room and pulled the drapes open enough to see Bryce's car in a different location than it had been when they'd had their hot make-out session. As she watched, the driver's door opened and Bryce got out.

She dropped the drape, feeling her stomach drop at the same time. It was true! He had gone back out after she had turned down his offer of sex and had gone after her daughter—her sweet daughter who had been enamored of him since the minute she saw him in the backyard. What had he done—plied her with alcohol that she wasn't legally old enough to drink, turned on the charm the way he had with her mother, then tried to go further than Dee wanted him to go? Or even worse, had he forced her into doing what he wanted? Lord knows his motor was probably still running on high after their episode in the car.

She flung open her front door and stomped out without closing it behind her. Bryce had just reached his own front door and was inserting his key in the lock. He turned, obviously surprised to see her.

"Laney?"

"You son-of-a-bitch! What did you do to my daughter?"

"I didn't do anything. . . ."

"Liar!" Laney heard her voice growing in volume and tried to get control of herself. It was still the middle of the night. While she wanted to scream and shout and hit the man standing before her, she also didn't want her neighbors to call the police. "Greg just called. Dee told him what you did."

"I didn't do anything, Laney—not like what you mean. I just. . . ."

"Save it. I don't want to hear your lies. I can't believe I almost fell for your bullshit! I can't believe I almost . . . just stay away from me and my daughter. Do you hear me? If you so much as look at either one of us . . . just stay away or I'll get a restraining order!"

She turned and headed back to her front door. She heard him say, "Laney, wait. Let me explain," then she slammed her front door, blocking out the sound of his voice. She leaned against the door, her entire body trembling, and felt the tears start to well. How could she have been so wrong about him? She didn't have a lot of experience with men, true, but to be *this* wrong? She had made a fool of herself, but worse, she had put her daughter in danger.

Her phone began to ring. She checked caller ID, saw it was a number she didn't recognize, and knew it was probably Bryce. She took the phone off the hook, depressed the button to disconnect the call, and left the handset on the counter. Greg and Dee both had her cell number if they needed to get in touch with her.

It was nearly four. She lay back down, knowing sleep was out of the question. As she lay there, she could not stop herself from remembering how it had felt to be held and kissed by him, and she began to cry.

***

She had finally fallen asleep just as the sky was starting to lighten and woke an hour later than she usually did. She started a pot of coffee. While it was brewing, she called Greg. If the grumpy tone of his voice was any indication, he had been sleeping late, too.

"How is Dee?" she said as soon as he answered.

"She's asleep."

"I want to talk to her."

"Why? So you can call her a liar?"

"So I can see if she's okay." Laney hesitated. "I apologize, Greg, for doubting what you said. After I hung up from you, I saw Bryce's car pull in next door. He had gone back out after dropping me off."

"Got great taste in men, don't you!"

What a perfect straight line, Laney thought, resisting the urge to point out that her lack of taste had started when she married him. This wasn't the time for petty squabbling.

"Let's not get into it, Greg," she said. "I told Bryce to stay away from both Dee and me, or I'd get a restraining order on him."

"Good for you." Greg sounded smug. "You should have listened to me from the beginning."

Greg had always enjoyed saying "I told you so" to her, but she'd come to realize since the divorce, that he'd always considered himself smarter than she was. It galled her to think that, in this case at least, he had been smarter. She had passed off his dislike of Bryce as simple jealousy, but maybe he had recognized the danger that Bryce posed. Women could see other women more clearly than men could see them, especially if the woman was gorgeous. Why wouldn't it be the same for men?

"I plan to get more than a restraining order on him," Greg continued. "I'm staying home today with Dee. I want to talk with her and find out exactly what went on. At the very least, he can be charged with supplying alcohol to an underage drinker. And if he tried anything with her, he can be charged with a lot more than that."

"Dee will have to do it, though," Laney said. "She's legally an adult. We can't bring charges on her behalf."

"Unfortunately. What we can do, though, is convince her to go through with it and support her when she does. She needs us together in her corner, Laney."

Laney was speechless for a moment. It was just like Greg to turn this whole sordid event into something he could use for his own benefit. She knew he was concerned for their daughter, but to try to weasel his way back into her good graces at the same time was low. She opened her mouth to tell him that, yes, she would be in Dee's "corner," but that didn't mean she'd be in his, but closed it again. It wasn't what was important now.

"I'll be at Rosedale today," she said. "Call me when Dee wakes up. I'll come over and we'll talk to her together."

Greg promised he would, and they hung up. Laney ate a quick breakfast of cereal and fruit, then showered and dressed for work. As she left, she saw that the blinds were still closed at the Davidsons. Apparently Bryce was sleeping late as well, likely worn out after the tomcatting he'd done during the night.

Greta had texted earlier to see if she was stopping at Starbucks, but Laney texted her back that she was running late. Since she was the boss, it didn't matter when she went into work, but the truth was, she wasn't ready to face Greta yet. She knew her friend was dying to hear what had transpired between her and Bryce after he took her home, and she just wasn't ready to talk about all of it yet. She needed to talk to Dee first.

She spent the morning scanning old files and receipts, all part of the cleanup she wanted to get done before the sale was finalized. The hours and minutes seemed to drag by while she waited for Greg's call. More than once, she started to call him, but stopped herself. Her daughter often slept until noon even when she hadn't been up all night. Greg had promised he would call after he talked with her, and Laney knew he'd keep that promise.

A little after eleven, the front desk called.

"There's a Mr. Rex Taylor here to see you," Patti said.

Laney had had so much on her mind that she'd completely forgotten Rex was stopping by. "I'll be right down," she said.

Rex was carrying on a lively conversation with two regular customers of the club whose names Laney couldn't think of at the moment. Based on what she caught of the conversation, it sounded like Rex had been asking them specifics about the club and how they liked it.

"There you are," he said. He kissed her lightly on the cheek. "Nice talking to you, guys."

The two men said their goodbyes, gathered their gear, and left. Rex turned back to Laney

"They seem to be satisfied customers," he said. "Had nothing but good to say about your club."

"I'm glad to hear it," she said. She handed him several guest passes. "I don't know how long you'll be in town, but if these aren't enough, feel free to ask for more."

"Thanks," he said. "Now, how about a tour?"

Laney showed him around, relieved to see that Greta was nowhere in sight. She had half-expected her friend to pop her head in the office and had been dreading her questions, but apparently Greta had other things on her plate that morning. Or maybe she was sleeping in, too. After all, it took both of them longer to recover from a night of partying than it used to take. They weren't kids anymore—even though Laney had been acting like one where Bryce was concerned.

Laney and Rex separated at the door to the men's locker room.

"I've got some things I need to do this afternoon or I'd ask you to a late lunch," he said. "Instead, how about dinner this evening?"

Laney hesitated. She might still be dealing with the Dee crisis, but she also wasn't crazy about being home alone this evening with Bryce next door. She didn't want to deal with his protestations of innocence.

"I think that will work," she said. "Although I may have to cancel at the last minute—a family thing. If all that's taken care of by evening, though, I'd be glad to have dinner with you."

"Great," Rex said. He took a business card and a pen from his inside suit pocket, scribbled something on the back of the card and handed it to her. "My personal cell number's on the back. If you can't make it, call me."

He smiled. He had kind of a cute smile, too, Laney realized suddenly. It was a lazy kind of smile, one that moved slowly across his face. And those eyes! Maybe dinner with him was just what she needed to get Bryce out of her thoughts.

"I hope you can make it," he said, his voice lowering. "Nothing I'd like better than to spend some time with you."

"I think I'd like that," she said.

"So, what time should I pick you up and where?"

She started to tell him she'd meet him somewhere. She didn't want to take the chance that Bryce might start a scene if he saw Rex and her together. Then she thought, why not? Let him see it. She had told him to stay away from her; maybe seeing her with Rex would make it clear to him that she meant it.

"How about six?" she said. "If you can spare another card, I'll write the address on the back for you."

"Sounds good," Rex said, handing her a card. "I'm looking forward to it."

"So am I," she said.

CHAPTER 8

Laney didn't usually spend all day at any of the clubs, but today she preferred looking at the four walls of her office rather than going home and dealing with Bryce. Greta had called her cell three times since noon, but Laney let it roll to voice mail. She wanted to talk to Dee before she talked to her friend about all that had happened.

The afternoon dragged on with no phone call from Greg. Finally at three, she couldn't stand it any longer. Maybe he hadn't talked to Dee yet, but if so, he could tell her that. She dialed his number, and he picked up on the third ring.

"Have you talked to Dee?" she said, not even bothering to say hello.

"We just finished a few minutes ago," Greg said. Laney was a little surprised to note that he sounded calm. "I was getting ready to call you."

"Is she there with you? Can you talk?"

"She's in the shower." Laney waited, but Greg didn't continue.

"Talk to me. What did she say? He didn't. . . ." Laney couldn't get the word "rape" out of her mouth, not in a conversation about her little girl. "Did he get her drunk and hurt her?"

"Apparently not," Greg said. "She was already drunk when she called him for a ride."

"When she what?"

"There was alcohol at the party. Everyone was drunk. Dee says she called Adams to come get her and her girlfriends and take them home."

"I don't understand. Why didn't she call one of us?"

"I guess she was hoping we wouldn't find out about her drinking. She thought we'd be in bed and she could sneak in."

Laney was silent for a few moments, processing what she'd just heard. Bryce hadn't gotten Dee drunk, but what had happened after he'd dropped her friends off? Something had upset her daughter.

"Did he do something to her after he dropped the other girls off?" she asked.

"She says not."

"Then why was she so upset?"

Greg was silent. Laney waited, wondering why he was acting so strangely. She had expected him to still be ranting and raving about what he was going to do to Bryce. Finally he spoke.

"She admitted she came on to him and he rebuffed her."

"What?"

"She's humiliated about the whole thing. It took me a while to get it out of her. She admitted she got his phone number while she was taking pictures with his phone at the party. She says she doesn't know why she did it, but then he refused her invitation to go with her and her friends, so after a few drinks . . . well, I guess it seemed like a good idea like a lot of things do after booze comes into play."

Laney flashed back to the party. Dee had turned away from them to take pictures of the buffet table and other guests with Bryce's phone and then her own cell had rung. Laney realized now that Dee had called her own phone with Bryce's, knowing that would leave a record of his number. She had known her daughter was attracted to Bryce, but she hadn't realized how much.

"So that's why she was crying last night," she said. "Embarrassment and hurt feelings."

"Magnified by too much alcohol."

"That still doesn't excuse Bryce," Laney said. "He should have knocked on my door and told me she needed a ride."

"Well, I won't argue with you there," Greg said. "But I guess she pretty much begged him not to tell you."

"You sound like you're defending him."

"Yeah, I guess I do," Greg said. "As much as I hate doing it. I still don't like the guy, and I'll be glad to see him go back to California, but he didn't take advantage of Dee. That's a point in his favor."

"I'm still at Rosedale," Laney said, "but I'll be leaving in a few minutes. Tell Dee I'll see her at home."

"Uh—she wants to stay here." Greg sounded funny, like there was something he wasn't telling her. "The girls are leaving on their road trip in a couple of days and she says she wants to stay with me until she goes."

"What? Why? I don't understand."

"I think she's just embarrassed," Greg said, but his tone said there was something more. He had never been a good liar. "Adams is staying next door to you, and naturally she wants to avoid him."

"Okay. Then I'll come by your place after I leave here."

"No." Greg spoke sharply. "That's probably not a good idea right now. She doesn't want to see you."

"She doesn't want to see me?" Laney couldn't believe what she was hearing. She and Dee had always been close. She'd been surprised that her daughter had chosen to go to her father's last night, but the news that Dee didn't want to see her was shocking.

"She's just embarrassed," Greg said again. "Give her a day or two."

"In a day or two, she'll be gone. What's going on, Greg? There's something else, isn't there? Something you're not telling me."

"Just give her some time, okay? I'll talk to her. Remember, she's humiliated and she's hung over, so she's not thinking straight today. I'll convince her she needs to see you before she goes. Please."

Laney hesitated. She badly wanted to see her daughter, to talk to her, to tell her everything would be all right, that every woman made a fool of herself over a man at some point in her life. The irony here was that both mother and daughter had made fools of themselves over the *same* man, but she decided she wouldn't mention that to Dee. Still, Greg was right. Dee was likely in pretty bad shape today. Maybe it would be best to give her another twenty-four hours to get back to normal.

"Okay," she finally agreed. "I won't push it today. But tell her I will see her tomorrow whether she likes it or not."

After they hung up, Laney sat in her office for several minutes, replaying the conversation. Greg hadn't told her everything, she was certain of that. But the important thing was that Bryce had not taken advantage of Dee, even though her daughter had offered him the opportunity. She had lambasted him for nothing. He should have woken her when Dee called, true, but that wasn't what she'd accused him of at his front door. The question now was what should she do about it.

The right thing to do was apologize, of course. But then what? Pick up where they had left off, and as soon as Dee had left on her road trip, hop in the sack? What if Dee somehow found out that the man she wanted had chosen her own mother instead? Greta had said her life was starting to sound like a soap opera, but Laney wasn't sure she wanted to star in a soap. Then again, Dee would be out-of-town for several weeks. By the time she got back, Bryce would be back in California. As long as they were discreet, there was no reason her daughter should find out.

Life had been so simple before Bryce Adams came to town and complicated her life with that crooked smile and his charm. She wished she had never known him as anything more than that sweet little boy she babysat when she was a teenager. She could stop what was growing between them, true, but it was too late to stop what she was feeling. She liked him, she wanted him, and even if what was developing between them didn't break her daughter's heart, it might very well break her own.

She sighed and stood. First things first—she had to apologize to Bryce. It was the right thing to do. Maybe she'd get lucky and he'd refuse to accept her apology. Maybe he'd decide it wasn't worth all the drama to get to snuggle with her again.

When she turned into her drive, she was surprised to see a strange car in the drive. Bryce's rental was nowhere to be seen. A new For Sale sign stood in the front lawn. A dark-haired woman who looked to be in her late fifties was knocking on the door. She turned as Laney pulled to a stop.

"Hi," she said when Laney had exited her car. "Do you happen to know if Mr. Adams is still in town?"

Laney nodded. "I think so."

"I'm Sheila Carpenter." The woman offered her business card. Laney glanced at it and saw it was for a real estate agency. "I knew Doris and Ed Davidson, the people who used to live here. Doris called me a couple of weeks ago and said her grandson would be coming back to list the house. He stopped by the office Friday afternoon and we filled out the paperwork. He said he didn't want a sign put up until he got the house fixed up a little, but he called early this morning and said he was ready for the sign. Said he might have to leave sooner than he'd planned."

"I don't know anything about that," Laney said past the lump that was building in her throat.

"Well, if you see him, tell him I stopped by. I'd hoped to get a look at the house, but I should have set up a definite time. I'll try to get him by phone." Sheila looked at Laney's house. "You've got a beautiful home here. If you ever want to put it on the market, give me a call."

"I'll remember that," Laney said, wishing the woman would leave.

"Nice meeting you," Sheila said and turned to her car.

Inside Laney leaned against the door, her heart pounding. Bryce was leaving! Apparently it was a sudden decision and she knew it had to be related to her accusations. She had threatened him with a restraining order, but she wondered if he was more concerned about legal charges. He had no way of knowing that Dee had come clean about what really happened. For all he knew, Dee was accusing him of sexual assault. Why didn't I wait, Laney thought. Why didn't I let him tell me his side of the story instead of acting like a mother bear, attacking first and asking questions later?

Her cell phone rang, interrupting her self-flagellation. The screen showed it was Greta. She answered immediately. She needed a girlfriend at this point.

"Hey," she said.

"Hey, back. Did you and Bryce just roll out of the sack or have you been avoiding me?"

"I've been avoiding you," Laney admitted.

"Well, I'm just around the corner so you can't avoid me anymore. I want details! Be there in five."

Laney smiled as she disconnected. Greta could always make her laugh, something she badly needed right about now. And Greta's no-nonsense way of looking at the world might help her gain some perspective on all that had happened. Better start the coffeemaker—this could take a while.

As she entered the kitchen, she saw that the message light on her answering machine was blinking. The counter showed she had three messages. She hit Play and Bryce's voice filled the small room. He sounded tense.

"Laney, please listen. I don't know what Dee told you, but I didn't touch her. She's a nice kid, but she is just a kid. She wanted me to come get her, and she begged me not to tell you. She sounded really scared, and she said she didn't want you upset. I should have come and told you—I know that now. I'm sorry. I wanted to tell you. . . ."

The tone sounded indicating the end of the message. He'd run out of time before he could finish it. The second message began playing.

"I wanted to explain to you in person," he continued. "But I have to go away for a few days. A friend called and wants me to take care of some business in St. Louis, so I'm catching a plane in an hour. I'm not sure how long it will take, but I should be back by the weekend. I'm. . . ."

Again, the tone sounded. As the third message began playing, she heard Greta's car pulling into the drive.

"I'm not giving up on us, Laney. Talk to Dee. Get her to tell you the truth." He paused, as if trying to think of what else he could say. "I'll see you when I get back."

This time he hung up before the time ran out on the message. Outside a car door slammed and a few seconds later, the front door opened and Greta called out, "It's me."

"In the kitchen," Laney called back while pouring water into the coffeemaker.

"So did you do it? How was it?" Greta was asking before she entered the kitchen. "I can't wait to hear all about it!"

"I'm not going to ask what 'it' is," Laney said, smiling.

Greta snorted. "If you have to ask, you're not the woman I thought you were. Come on—don't keep me in suspense. Did you or did you not go 'all the way' with Bryce." She put finger quotes in the air around "all the way."

Laney set the carafe on the burner, hit the Start button, and turned to Greta.

"It's a long story," she said.

***

"Wow!" Greta said when Laney finished. "So you really gave him hell for nothing?"

"He should have called me instead of going to get Dee himself." Laney recognized it was a weak defense. "But, yeah, basically I did."

"Have you heard from him since?"

"He left a message—messages—on the machine." She motioned with her head toward the answering machine on the counter.

"May I?" Greta paused with her finger poised over the Play button. Laney nodded and Greta hit Play. After the third message had finished, they sat in silence for a moment, sipping their coffee.

"Wonder what the 'business' is?" Greta's comment surprised Laney. She had expected her friend to focus instead on Bryce's statement that he wasn't giving up. Laney hadn't paid much attention to the business comment on either the first or second hearing, but Greta had a point. What "business" had pulled Bryce away so suddenly?

"I don't know," she said. "I hadn't thought about it when I first listened to the messages, but you're right. He's being kind of secretive about it, isn't he?"

"Well, maybe he just didn't want to waste message time on it. Obviously he was more interested in protesting his innocence to you."

"Or maybe it's something he doesn't want me to know." Unable to sit still, Laney began to pace the kitchen. "I mean, what do I know about him, Greta? I know he's a gorgeous hunk and seems like a nice guy, but he's a thirty-year-old man who apparently doesn't have a job. For all I know, he's transporting drugs to St. Louis for his friend—or for himself."

"Oh, come on," Greta said. "You knew his family. They're not like that."

"And you know a good upbringing doesn't guarantee a child won't go bad. Think about how many families we know with parents who are good people and kids who are messed up on drugs."

"Okay," Greta nodded. "I'll give you that. But Bryce looks way too healthy to be a druggie."

"So maybe he doesn't use. Maybe he just sells."

"Stop it." Greta raised her hands, palm out. "You know what you're doing, don't you? You're trying to talk yourself out of Bryce Adams because he's the first guy to break through the shell you put up after Greg did a number on you."

Laney stopped pacing and stared at Greta.

"That's not it," she started, but Greta interrupted.

"Yes, it is. First, you had a problem with the age difference, and then you jumped to the conclusion that he'd done something to Dee before you heard what she had to say. Now you're ready to label him a drug kingpin—again before you know the facts. You want the guy and it scares the hell out of you. Doesn't it?"

Laney sighed and collapsed onto the stool. "You really think that's what I'm doing?"

"I do."

"Well, even if I am, Greta, you know getting involved with Bryce is a bad idea."

"And why is that?"

"Besides the fact that he's too young for me, Dee would be hurt and humiliated if she found out. Greg has already made a fool of himself and would probably go nuclear if Bryce and I became involved. And last but not least, Bryce will go back to California."

"The way I see it, his going back to California takes care of the first two objections. Neither Dee nor Greg has to find out." Greta's voice grew soft. "Sweetie, it sounds to me like you're afraid of falling hard for the guy, only to have him leave. That's why you're trying to talk yourself out of him."

"So what if that is it?" Laney said. "I'm not saying it is, but if it was, wouldn't that be a good enough reason to avoid getting anything started?"

"Honey, I've seen you two together. It's already started. Besides, there are no guarantees in any relationship. Even if Bryce was born the same year you were, Dee thought he was an old fuddy-duddy, Greg liked him, and he was a hometown boy, it still doesn't mean things would work out long term. If you won't take a chance on a man unless he comes with a guarantee, you're gonna be waiting a long time."

"So you think I should apologize then?"

"Honey, I think you should kiss and make up." Greta grinned. "And then keep going. You want to get something to eat tonight? We can continue this conversation over a few drinks."

"I can't." Laney hadn't told her about Rex. "I have a date."

"You what?"

"Rex came by the club today and asked me to dinner. I still thought Bryce had done something to Dee and I didn't know Bryce had left town. I thought if he saw me with Rex, he'd leave me alone. I did warn Rex that I might have to cancel, though, so maybe. . . ."

"Don't you dare." Greta shook her head. "Just because I've been encouraging you to take a chance on Bryce doesn't mean you should limit your options. Rex is a hunk, too. Maybe you'll find you like him better than Bryce. Now, let's go pick out what you're going to wear."

CHAPTER 9

Rex showed up a few minutes before six dressed in white pants and sports coat, and a blue shirt—no surprise there. He smiled that slow smile when she opened the door, and she had to admit it did give her a little tingle. Greta was right—he was easy on the eyes.

"Joanna and Bill recommended Jonathan's," he said after they'd gotten into his car. "I made reservations, but if you'd rather go somewhere else, we can."

"Jonathan's is fine. They have great food."

They chitchatted about the weather and the town on their way to the restaurant. As they entered the restaurant, Rex casually placed his hand on the small of her back to guide her through the door ahead of him. She couldn't help but compare the way it made her feel to the way she felt when Bryce touched her. Bryce's touch never failed to ignite a fire in her that she had thought long extinguished, but it also made her uncomfortable in public. She felt like everyone was watching and judging her for being with a younger man. In contrast, Rex's touch was simply comfortable and reassuring. There was no embarrassment associated with an older man touching his younger companion. She supposed her attitude was old-fashioned, but it was what it was.

Rex asked for a booth and the hostess led them to a secluded table in a corner. A waiter appeared within seconds with menus and took their drink orders. Rex asked for Johnnie Walker Black on the rocks; she ordered wine. They were still perusing the extensive menu when the waiter brought their drinks, and he left to give them a few more minutes. After a little discussion about what Laney knew to be good, Rex decided on the scallops and Laney chose the roasted salmon. They settled back with their drinks.

"So—Joanna and Bill tell me you and your ex are selling your clubs," Rex said.

Laney nodded. If Rex was the buyer, he had apparently decided not to reveal that information over dinner. She could see it from his point of view. While it was never a wise business decision to talk to a seller without a third-party present, it also could add an unwanted layer of tension to a personal night out.

"We should finalize the sale any day now," she said. "The buyer's people have been doing their due diligence the last few weeks. It shouldn't be long before they're finished."

"How do you feel about giving up something you created?"

"Relieved," she said. "*Very* relieved. I'm ready for a change."

"I imagine it's difficult to be partners with an ex-spouse," Rex said. "I doubt I could do it."

"I don't think I asked—do you have children?"

"No, thank goodness. I don't have anything against kids—in fact, I think I would have liked to have had a couple. But I would not want anything tying me to my ex-wife."

"That bad, huh?"

"Let's just say she's a difficult person," Rex said. He smiled. "A lot like your ex-husband, I suspect."

"How long were you married?"

"Just three years. I think I knew after one that it wasn't going to last, but it took me two more to make the break."

"How old were you?"

"I was thirty-eight when we got married."

"Wow. You were a late bloomer."

"Stayed too busy with work until then. It's hard to keep any relationship going when you're away from home a lot on business. And it's just as hard on a marriage." He smiled that slow lazy smile and raised his glass to her. "Traveling all the time can be a pain, but sometimes it does lead you to someone you'd like to get to know better."

She smiled and raised her glass in a toast. He was almost as good as Bryce at turning on the charm. It looked like it was going to be an enjoyable evening.

***

The food was good, the wine excellent, and the company even better. During dinner, they talked about their lives and the people in them. Rex asked a few questions about Bodies, but kept them to a minimum. Considering his background in business, his lack of interest was suspicious in itself. As the buyer, he would already know a lot about Bodies. If he weren't the buyer, Laney would have expected him to show more interest. Then again, maybe he simply preferred not mixing business with pleasure.

"Would you like to go somewhere for a nightcap?" Rex said. They were waiting for the waiter to return with his card and the charge printout for him to sign. "Or better yet, for dancing, since I didn't get the chance to do as much of that as I would have liked last night."

"Sorry about that." Laney felt herself blushing. "Greg was an ass."

"Well, the only benefit to his jealous tantrum was that Adams didn't get to dance with you much either." Rex was smiling, a teasing look in his eyes. "So—is there some place you'd like to go?"

"There's a club on the south edge of town that has dancing, but it's the kind of place that attracts the twenty-somethings," Laney said. "Loud, noisy, and crowded. That's about it."

"Well, then, I'll guess we'll just have to settle for the nightcap. I'm staying at the Westgate. Their lounge is nice and it's not loud."

The Westgate was the best hotel in the city. Rex was right. The lounge was nice and locals, as well as travelers, frequented it for its soft lights, good drinks, private booths, and subdued music. It was a good choice for an after-dinner drink. It was also in the same building as Rex's bed and that could be a problem. Then again, they were both adults. He wasn't going to force her into anything she didn't want to do.

"One drink," she said.

"One it will be," he agreed, but the look in his eyes said he fully intended to do his best to keep the night from ending there.

The Lounge at the Westgate had two main entrances, one to the street and another to the lobby. The lobby entrance had a thick door with opaque glass inserts that effectively blocked the bright lights and bustle of the lobby. The lighting was low, the carpet thick, and the layout of booths, dividers, and potted plants—all artificial—designed for maximum privacy. A third door was placed discreetly at the end of the hall leading to the bathrooms. Elevators were located around a corner from the lobby desk and the lounge's third door opened directly across from them, providing guests who wanted a drink access to the lounge without crossing the lobby. It also provided lounge patrons quick access to the rooms while ensuring maximum privacy.

The lounge was nearly empty, and Laney didn't recognize any of the people there. Locals frequented the place more on weekends or just after work on weekdays. The few patrons were probably people staying at the hotel or people from surrounding towns meeting someone they didn't want their neighbors to know about. Rex led her to a high-backed booth in an alcove far from the lobby door and slid in beside her. She ordered another wine and he ordered another Scotch.

As they waited for their drinks, he put his arm around her shoulders, leaned in, and kissed her lightly on the lips.

"I've wanted to do that since Bill introduced us," he said. "Hope you don't mind."

Laney smiled. "No, I don't mind."

The waitress arrived with their drinks, and they sipped in silence for a few moments. A Frank Sinatra tune was playing, but Laney couldn't identify the title. She knew she knew the song, but she couldn't concentrate on anything but the feel of Rex's arm across her shoulders, the muscles of his thighs straining against his pants, and the fact that his room was right upstairs. All she had to do was say the word, and they would be in the elevator on their way to what would likely be a very pleasurable night. And that's all it would be. She and Rex could enjoy each other for a few days and nights, he would conclude his business, whether or not it involved Bodies, and he would go home to Atlanta. No commitments, no complications, and no broken hearts.

The Sinatra tune ended and a slow instrumental Laney wasn't familiar with began playing. Rex slid his arm down from her shoulders, took her hand, and slid out of the booth.

"How about that dance?" he said.

No one was seated near them, and the dividers that formed the alcove provided privacy from the other patrons. Only the bartender had a view of their booth and the open space beside it. It would be almost like dancing alone, Laney thought, feeling a little tingle of anticipation. She slid out of the booth and into Rex's arms.

He pulled her close, pressing her against his body. His broad back felt strong and safe under her left hand; her right was wrapped securely in his, their clasped hands pulled in against his chest. His hips moved slightly against her in time to the music, and she felt a tantalizing bulge against her leg. She pressed her face against his neck, breathed in deeply of his light cologne, and sighed. He pulled his head back slightly and kissed her, his tongue penetrating her lips, slowly, teasingly, their bodies still moving with the music.

She felt a rush of desire. How had she gone three years without a man's kiss, more than three, really, since it had been a long time since Greg kissed her this way. The warmth and strength of a man's body against her own, the hungry demand communicated by the press of a man's lips and exploring tongue—she hadn't known how much she had missed it all until Bryce kissed her in his car. His lips, his eyes, his cute crooked smile, the feel of him beneath her as she straddled him in the front seat of the rental car like a teenager with her boyfriend in her family's driveway. . . .

Suddenly she was fully present in the lounge, aware she and Rex were not alone, that she was "making love with clothes on," as Greta liked to say, in a public place. She pulled away from his kiss. He resisted for a moment before letting her go.

"Wow!" she said with a nervous laugh. "I think we're getting a little carried away."

"I'm enjoying it." Rex started to nuzzle her neck, but she stepped back just as the music ended.

"There are people around."

He was still holding her hand and now he took the other one as well. "Then let's go where there aren't any," he said.

Laney looked at him for a few moments, still tempted, but not enough. She shook her head.

"I'd better not," she said. "I really need to get home."

"I'd take you home in the morning." He tried to pull her close again, but she resisted.

"I really can't, Rex. I'm sorry. My daughter would wonder where I was."

Kids sure come in handy, Laney thought, feeling only a little guilty at the white lie. It was easier than trying to explain. Suddenly she remembered the name of the Sinatra song that had been playing when they'd walked into the lounge. It was Something Stupid. Appropriate, she thought, although not in the meaning of the song lyrics. She'd just done something that was probably stupid. She had turned this man down, not because he wasn't handsome or sexy or, as far as she knew, a nice human being, but only because he wasn't Bryce Adams.

CHAPTER 10

Tuesday morning, Laney was up at her usual time of six-thirty even though she'd had trouble falling asleep after Rex dropped her off. She hadn't been able to shut off the thoughts that bounced around in her brain. Bryce dominated her thoughts, but Rex claimed his share. After the kiss in the lounge and another in the car in her drive, it was impossible not to think of him.

Rex hadn't been happy about her refusal to go upstairs with him, but he'd been gracious and accepted it. They had finished their drinks sitting close to one another in the booth, thigh to thigh, his arm around her. It had felt comfortable and secure, yet at the same time, an undercurrent of sexual tension was there. He was a handsome man, but more than that, he had an air of confidence that was incredibly sexy.

"Don't suppose you've changed your mind?" he'd asked, a twinkle in his eyes, when they'd finished their drinks and stood to leave.

She'd smiled and shook her head. "I can't, Rex. I'm sorry."

"No problem. Just thought I'd ask."

He escorted her to the door leading to the sidewalk, his hand resting on her back. What is it with guys and the hand on the back, she wondered? Was it something in their genetic makeup—a way to mark a female they wanted to claim as a mate? An image of a hairy and hunched caveman with his hand on the back of an equally hairy and hunched cavewoman flashed into her mind, and she stifled the urge to laugh.

"I have to run up to Cincinnati tomorrow afternoon and probably won't be back until late Wednesday," he said after they were in the car. "Since I wasn't able to talk you into staying over for breakfast, how about we get lunch before I leave?"

Laney hesitated for a second. Was it a good idea to encourage Rex by continuing to see him when she knew she wasn't going to let it develop into anything? Bryce had come out the winner in this competition the two men seemed to have going. On the other hand, maybe Greta was right. Maybe she should keep her options open. She liked Rex, he was gorgeous and sexy and successful, and he wasn't eleven years younger than she was. All in all, he was the more logical choice.

"I'd like that," she said. "What time is good for you?"

"How's eleven-thirty?"

"That will work," she said. "I plan on going into the Rosedale club for a few hours in the morning."

"I planned on working out so I'll meet you there."

That settled, they drove the rest of the way in companionable silence. He turned in her drive, and put the car in Park, leaving the motor running. He turned to her.

"In case you haven't figured it out by now, I like you, lady." He reached out and brushed her hair back from her face, that slow lazy smile moving across his face. "You're smart, good-looking, and sexy as hell."

"That's funny," she said. "I was thinking the same thing about you."

He pulled her to him and kissed her. It was like his smile, a slow kiss that grew in intensity without rushing, taking its time and getting it right. It's probably the way he makes love, Laney thought, and felt a rush of warmth.

"I don't plan on giving up," he said, murmuring the words against her lips, then kissed her again.

By the time they separated, Laney wasn't sure she had the strength to walk to her door. He gave her a final quick peck on the forehead, then got out and came around to her side, opened the passenger door, and extended his hand. She took it, glad for something to hold onto until she was sure she was steady enough to walk. Weak in the knees, she thought. That's what he's done to me—made me weak in the knees.

At her front door, he kissed her again, but it was a casual friendly kiss, the kind of kiss that wouldn't raise the eyebrows of any nosy neighbors who happened to be watching. Of course, if they'd been watching long enough to see the kiss in the car, their eyebrows would already be at their hairline.

"I had a great time tonight," Laney said.

"So did I." He smiled, his eyes twinkling. "Even if it did end sooner than I'd have liked."

She laughed. "Well, goodnight. See you tomorrow."

"Looking forward to it."

She stood in the door, watching until he started his car, then gave him a little wave and went inside. She did all the get-ready-for-bed things she always did, then lay looking at the darkened ceiling. Her body still tingled from that slow kiss in the car, but when she thought of Bryce's kisses and his body pressed against hers that warm tingle ignited into a fire. She wanted them both physically, but something about Bryce . . . was it the "forbidden" aspect of an older woman and a younger man? Forbidden only in her mind, of course, since society didn't seem to mind all that much. Well, maybe some segments of it might—like her daughter. Rex was the safer choice. Dee liked him, but she didn't lust for him the way she did Bryce. And it wasn't as if choosing Rex would be like settling for the booby prize.

She got up and got a glass of water, then lay back down and closed her eyes. A minute later, they popped open again. Maybe she was overthinking the entire thing. After all, it wasn't as if she was in the market for a husband or even a boyfriend. If that were the case, then Rex doubtless would be the better choice—or at least the more logical one. He was the right age—at least as far as she was concerned, old fuddy-duddy that she was—and he was successful. Bryce was eleven years younger—a few more years and the difference would be that of mother and son—and he didn't seem to be setting the world on fire financially. But since she wasn't looking for anything permanent, a promising outlook for the future of the relationship wasn't really an issue. In fact, that made Bryce the better choice. Rex was at an age where a man is often ready to settle down. He might be the one to get serious. She and Bryce could have a fling, and he would go back to California. Everything would go back to the way it was before these two men had turned her world topsy-turvy by their arrival in town.

Of course, there was Dee to think of, but she would be leaving for her road trip. Bryce would probably be back on the west coast by the time Dee came home. She would never have to know that her mother had had a midlife crisis that involved jumping Bryce's bones. It could work out. Still, Rex certainly was one hell of a kisser. . . . It was well after midnight when Laney finally fell asleep.

The house phone rang just as she finished her bowl of oatmeal. It was Dee.

"Hey, Mom. Hope I didn't wake you."

"Nope. I just finished breakfast." Laney hesitated, wondering if she should broach the subject of the Bryce episode or wait for Dee to bring it up. Finally, she settled for, "How are you, honey?"

"I'm okay." Was that embarrassment in her daughter's voice? "Are you going to be around this morning? I'd like to come over and get packed for the trip, but I wanted to talk to you, too."

"I was getting ready to leave for Rosedale," Laney said. "But I can do that this afternoon. When will you be here?"

"I can come over now, if that's okay."

"That's fine. I'll fix pancakes."

Laney hung up and breathed a huge sigh of relief. She hadn't realized how worried she'd been that her daughter would leave on her road trip without talking to her. In the back of her mind had been the irrational worry that something would happen to Dee on the trip and she'd never see her baby again. She began gathering and mixing the ingredients for chocolate chip pancakes, Dee's favorite. She would let the batter sit until Dee got there to give the baking powder time to do its thing.

"Hey, baby. I'm in the kitchen," she called when she heard Dee's key in the front door.

"Hi, Mom." Dee crossed to where Laney stood at the counter and kissed her on the cheek. "Ummm— chocolate chip! Just what I wanted!"

"I already had oatmeal, but I think I've got room for a couple of these myself." Laney oiled the electric griddle and turned it on. "Coffee?"

They sipped their coffee while the griddle heated, making small talk about the weather, how Jana was doing after her bout with food poisoning, what Dee should pack for the trip. The buzzer sounded, indicating the griddle was ready, and Laney dropped six ladles of batter onto the surface, watching as it spread out. The question was still hanging in the air—bring up Bryce or just let it drop and enjoy a pleasant morning with her daughter. By the time the pancakes were done, she'd decided on the latter course of action.

While they ate, they continued talking about what Dee should pack and where the girls planned to go first, but Laney thought Dee seemed distracted. After they finished the pancakes, Dee rinsed the plates and put them in the dishwasher, while Laney cleaned the griddle. Laney poured each of them another cup of coffee and they sat back down on their stools facing one another.

"Are you okay, honey?" Laney asked.

"Yeah, I'm okay," Dee said. "I'm just embarrassed about the other night. I know Dad told you what happened."

Laney nodded. "He did. But it's nothing to be embarrassed about. You shouldn't have been drinking, but you know that without my telling you. I'm just glad you weren't hurt."

"I know Dad told you I called Bryce."

"Yes, and I wish you would have trusted me enough to call me."

"I know I should have," Dee said, finding something interesting in her coffee so she didn't have to look at Laney. "It's so embarrassing."

"Look." Laney took Dee's hand. "I know what happened, okay? I know you like him and I know you told him that. I'm just thankful that he didn't take advantage of you in that situation."

Dee raised her eyes and looked at Laney. "Did Dad tell you why Bryce turned me down?"

"Well, not in so many words, but I assumed it was because you were drunk, you're young, and he was enough of a gentleman to not take advantage of the situation."

"That might have been part of it," Dee said. "But that's not the reason he gave."

"What do you mean? What was the reason?"

"He turned me down because he's in love with you."

Laney's mouth dropped open as she stared at her daughter, trying to think of a reply. "What?" she finally managed to get out.

"He's in love with you."

"He said that?"

"Well, not those exact words. He said he was crazy about you and that pretty much means the same thing, don't you think?"

Laney dropped her daughter's hand and stood, moving to the coffeemaker to top off her cup of coffee that didn't need topping off. She needed the time to get her heart rate back down to normal.

"Are you sure you didn't misunderstand?" she said, her back still to her daughter. "You'd had a lot to drink apparently."

"I didn't have a blackout, Mom." Dee sounded a little exasperated. "I know what he said. And I'm worried about you."

"Worried?" One surprise after another, Laney thought, turning to look at her daughter. "Why are you worried?"

"Well, first I have to admit I was pretty upset with you. And embarrassed about it all. I mean, he is a lot younger than you, right? It's kind of embarrassing to think of your mom as a cougar. I was going to come get my stuff while you were at Bodies and just leave on the trip."

"What changed your mind? Wait, before you answer that—there is nothing going on between Bryce and me. I just want you to know that."

"That's not what Dad says." It was obvious Dee didn't believe her. "And why would Bryce say something like that if nothing was going on?"

"Your father is jealous and paranoid," Laney said, choosing to ignore the question about why Bryce said what he did. Best defense is a good offense, she thought. Besides, Greg *is* jealous and paranoid. "He saw us dancing at the Millers and jumped to the wrong conclusion."

"You danced with Mr. Taylor, too, didn't you? Dad didn't say anything about him."

Damn you, Greg, Laney thought.

"He didn't like it," Laney said. "But the Millers think Rex might be our buyer. That's the only reason your father didn't object to my dancing with him. For that matter," she added, "I went to dinner with Rex last night."

"Bryce won't like that," Dee muttered.

"Dee!" Laney spoke sharply.

"I'm sorry. I shouldn't have said that." Dee sighed. "But I am worried about you. And so is Dad. After he and I talked last night, I thought it over and decided I owed it to you to come talk to you before you made a huge mistake."

"I'm not following. What *are* you talking about? What mistake do you think I'm about to make? Or maybe I should say, what *mistake* has your father convinced you I'm about to make?"

Laney said the last with bitterness. Ever since the divorce and even during the turmoil leading up to it, she had always made a point of never using a critical tone when talking about Greg with their daughter. Greg had a lot of faults, but he was a good father. Dee loved him and Laney wanted her to continue to love him. Dee didn't know about Greg's affairs; they had only told her that they had grown apart. It irked her that now Greg was seeding their daughter's mind with his suspicions about her relationship with Bryce.

"Dad is worried about you, Mom. Just like I am." Dee was beginning to sound more than a little patronizing. Laney wanted to ask her just who the mother was, but she bit her tongue. Her baby was going to leave on a road trip and Laney didn't want their last conversation together to turn into an argument.

"But why are you worried?" Laney said. "I told you nothing is going on with Bryce, but even if it were, why would that worry you?"

"Because he's after your money."

"What? My money! What in God's name are you talking about?"

"Think about it, Mom. When you and Dad sell the clubs, you're going to be kind of rich. Bryce is just a massage therapist. If he's even working."

"Is this coming from your Dad?"

"Dad figured it out, yeah, but I agree with him. Let's face it, Mom. You don't exactly have a lot of experience with men. You were married to Dad, like, forever. Bryce is a hunk who could have any woman he wanted."

"So why would he want me? Is that what you're saying?"

"Mom!" Dee dragged the word out in that way all young girls did when exasperated with their mothers. "You know what I mean. You said he was too old for me. Well, you're too old for him. So why's he going after you? Your money, that's why."

Laney stared at her daughter, thinking how much she would like to murder the girl's father. Was Greg using Dee to try to put a damper on the attraction for Bryce he had spotted growing in Laney? Or did he really believe this ridiculous fiction just like he believed the fiction he had told himself about their chances for a future together.

"Dee, I need to explain something to you," Laney said, trying to maintain a reasonable tone when what she really wanted to do was scream and shout and throw things. "Somehow your father has come to believe that we can get back together. I have told him there's no chance of that, but he refuses to believe it. He is jealous of Bryce, because he still sees me as 'his.' He doesn't want to see me with anyone else, so he manufactures this . . . this, I don't know . . . conspiracy theory about Bryce being after my money. That's all it is."

"Dad told me he still loves you and wants to make your marriage work. Why won't you give him a chance?"

The tone of Dee's voice and the look in her eyes were that of a small child who can't understand why her mommy and daddy want to break up her family. Laney's heart nearly broke as she looked at her daughter. Had she made a mistake by not telling Dee what had really led to the divorce? She had been old enough three years ago to know the truth. But then again, what was the truth really? Yes, Greg had cheated, but hadn't their marriage been in its death throes long before that? The truth was the adultery had been a symptom, not the cause, of all that was wrong in their relationship. What they had told Dee—that they had grown apart—had been the truth.

"Dee, I'm sorry. I know you'd like your father and me to get back together, but it's not going to happen. I don't hate your father. I even love him in a way—for what we had at one time and because of you. But I don't love him the way a wife needs to love a husband. I've moved on. I thought he had as well, but I guess he's had enough of being single and wants to settle down. That's great—but it won't be with me."

"Because you're too busy having a fling with your boy-toy!"

"Oh, my God! I know you got that from your father, because he used the same words with me!" Laney slammed her fist down on the counter. Dee jumped and looked at her wide-eyed. "Bryce is not my 'boy-toy.' He's a nice young man who comes from a nice family. There is nothing going on between us, regardless of what your father thinks."

"And," she added, unable to stop herself, "if there were, it would be my business. I'm forty-one years old and don't need my ex-husband or my daughter telling me who I can or cannot date! Do you understand?"

Dee stared at her coffee cup, not meeting Laney's eyes.

"Do you?" Laney demanded.

"Yes," Dee whispered. "I'm sorry. I'm just worried about you, that's all."

That wasn't all, Laney knew. Dee was embarrassed and hurt by Bryce's rejection of her advances. She needed a reason to hate him for wounding her ego, and Greg had been more than happy to give her one that he hoped would further his own agenda. Now Dee had convinced herself that her mother was the target of a con man.

"I know, baby." Laney took her daughter in her arms and hugged her tight. "I appreciate your concern, but you have to learn to balance concern with meddling. It's a balancing act I have to do every day with you. I didn't like you wearing that skimpy bathing suit to the Millers. A few years ago, I could have forbidden you to leave the house in it, but you're an adult now and I have to learn to keep my mouth shut. It's not easy, believe me, but adults have to respect and honor each other's boundaries. I have to respect yours, but you—as an adult—have to also respect mine."

She pulled back and kissed Dee on the forehead.

"Okay?"

Dee nodded, her eyes wet. "Okay. I'll try. Just be careful, okay?"

"I will," Laney said. "I promise. Now, we'd better get started on that packing, don't you think?"

CHAPTER 11

Laney barely made it to Bodies before Rex arrived to pick her up for lunch. After the conversation with Dee over pancakes, she'd helped her daughter choose what to take with her on her trip. That ate up most of the morning, since neither was good at packing light. After Dee left, Laney had poured another cup of coffee and sat on her patio thinking about what Dee had said.

It hadn't occurred to her that she would be—as Dee put it—"kind of rich" after the sale was final. She knew the numbers, of course, and had realized it was a good price and she wouldn't need to worry about finding a job, but rich? She wouldn't be in the same category as Bill Gates or a Walton, but she would have enough to live comfortably for the rest of her life, especially since she didn't carry a mortgage on her house.

Was that money going to prove to be a curse more than a blessing, she wondered now? From this point forward, would she have to be suspicious of any man who showed an interest in her? She didn't believe Bryce was after her money. Greg and Dee were wrong about that. He didn't seem like the kind of person who cared all that much about money as long as he had enough for the basics. No, he wasn't after her money, but she didn't want to tell her daughter that she knew what he *was* after.

She had closed her eyes and leaned back in the Adirondack chair, her body growing warm, not from the June sun, but from thoughts of Bryce. It took very little effort to remember the way he had felt pressed against her on the dance floor and in the car as she straddled him. Her lips moved slightly as she unconsciously responded to the memory of his kiss. It was as if his touch and kisses were imprinted on her. While she could remember how good Rex's kisses had felt, that was more a pleasant memory, much like the memory of what she'd had to eat when they went to dinner. The way Bryce felt had become a part of her at a cellular level.

Rex! What time was it? She stood quickly, glancing at her watch. She hurriedly brushed the pancakes out of her teeth, applied makeup, and dressed. Thankfully, she'd showered before Dee had arrived, and her hair had dried. One of the benefits of naturally curly hair, she decided. Even though it could sometimes get unruly, it usually didn't require more than shampoo, conditioner, and a warm day to dry quickly.

She'd been in her office no more than twenty minutes when the desk called to say Rex had arrived. Today he was wearing a gray business suit that complemented the gray streaks in his hair, a white shirt, and—no surprise—a blue tie. He did know how to dress to look his best, she thought, not that he needed to make the effort. He would have looked good no matter what he was wearing. He probably looked even better wearing nothing at all. She smiled at the thought, and he looked at her questioningly, that slow smile starting to spread across his face.

"What?" he said.

She shrugged. "Nothing. Just glad to see you."

"You looked like you had something very nice on your mind just then," he murmured as they exited the front door of Bodies. "Sure you wouldn't like to share?"

"I don't know what you're talking about," she said, smiling, and he laughed.

"I took the liberty of making a reservation at the Moonglow," Rex said. "I hope that's okay."

Laney nodded. "That's fine. They have really good food."

And low lights and private booths, Laney thought, but didn't say. It was the same café where Bryce had wanted to take her for lunch that first day. She had felt awkward about going to such an intimate place with a man so much younger than she, but Rex was different. Damn, she thought. Trying to decide between these two men is as difficult as deciding between two gorgeous pairs of shoes! Although, she thought, a woman can always buy both pairs of shoes. Two men—now that would be asking for trouble! Wouldn't it?

She stopped in her tracks, shocked by the fact that she was even considering such a thing. What was wrong with her? She had spent over two decades sleeping with the same man, then three years sleeping alone, and now the possibility of sleeping with two had actually crossed her mind! Maybe she should make an appointment with her doctor and have her hormone levels checked. Maybe being pursued by two desirable males had thrown her glands into overdrive.

"Something wrong?" Rex said.

"No. Of course not." She started walking again. "It . . . I mean, I just thought of something I'd forgotten to do this morning. I can take care of it later."

Rex seemed to believe her little white lie. They continued walking the block to the Moonglow, making small talk about the weather.

The usual lunch crowd hadn't arrived yet, and they were escorted to a preferred booth at the rear of the restaurant. Laney couldn't help but notice the similarity of it to their booth at the Westgate the night before. Both were private and located away from prying eyes. She wondered if Rex had specified those attributes when he made the lunch reservation. She wouldn't put it past him.

He took the seat across from her in the booth instead of sliding in beside her like he had the night before. Both ordered coffee from the waitress, perused their menus, and were ready to place their orders when their drinks arrived. After the waitress had taken their food orders and left, Rex leaned forward and took Laney's hand.

"You know I hate like hell to leave right now, don't you?" he said.

Laney could feel herself starting to blush. "Business is business," she said.

"Unfortunately true," he said. "I'm glad you understand. A lot of women don't. You're different, though, because you have a successful business yourself."

"Not for much longer, thank goodness!" She laughed, relieved that the conversation had moved to more neutral ground.

"Have you given any thought to what you'll do after the sale?"

"Um, I dunno. Sleep?"

He laughed. "I hear that. What I meant was, do you plan on staying here?"

"Well, yes, I guess." The question came as a surprise. Laney hadn't thought about the fact that she would no longer be tied to the town. Dee had flown the nest, so once Bodies was no longer her concern, there would be nothing stopping her from going elsewhere. "I really haven't thought about it. I've lived here all my life, and my friends are here. I'm sure I'll travel more, of course."

"Maybe you'll come see me in Atlanta." That slow smile again—Lordy, that is sexy, Laney thought.

"Maybe I will," she said.

After Bryce went back to California, maybe a trip to Georgia would be in order. After all, that wasn't quite the same thing as trying to juggle two men at once, was it? Could she have her cake and eat it, too? She fought the urge to giggle, knowing Rex would think she was acting like a silly schoolgirl because he'd invited her to Atlanta.

"You know," she said. "I've never asked you—what kind of businesses do you have? I mean, Joanna said you and your partners have several businesses, but not what kind."

"I've been in business with two other guys for close to twenty years now," he said. We have a few shopping centers, most in the Midwest and South, but a couple in Arizona. That's how we started. Bought one that was in bankruptcy, did okay with that, and kept going. We're just starting to branch out into other types of businesses."

Like fitness clubs, she wondered, but didn't say. If he was their buyer and he wanted to tell her, he would.

If not, it would probably be circumspect of her not to bring it up. In a couple of weeks—at most—she would learn the buyer's identity anyway.

While they ate, he told her a little about how he and his partners got started. They had become friends while working for NCR at the company headquarters in Atlanta. One of them had heard of a strip mall whose owner was having financial difficulties. They had pooled their money and credit to buy it and never looked back.

Such a difference between the two men responsible for her current hormone imbalance, Laney thought. Rex not only was older, he was a poster boy for the American dream, not just successful, but very likely wealthy. Bryce was a massage therapist and, as far as she could tell, seemed content with his lot in life. Of course, he was still young and that might change, but somehow Laney doubted it.

Rex had asked her if she had given any thought to what she might do after the sale of Bodies and she had told him the truth. She hadn't given it any thought. Now, as she listened to him talk, it dawned on her that she could do just about anything she wanted. With the money she would clear from the sale, she could support her current lifestyle for the rest of her life without working, but if she made wise investments, she really would be "kind of rich." She could relocate, she could buy or build a bigger house, she could travel. Greta had the money and time to jet around with her. They'd taken a few girls-only trips already; Laney knew Greta would be up for many more. She could even visit handsome successful men in Atlanta—or laidback massage therapists in California.

For the first time in her life, she was completely free to do whatever she wanted. No husband, no small child, and plenty of money. The realization left her feeling giddy, as if she'd drunk a little too much wine with lunch instead of one cup of coffee. She heard everything Rex said, made witty comments at just the right moment, laughed and joked, while her mind whirled with the possibilities that lay before her, not the least of which was the sexy hunk seated across from her. She toyed with the idea of suggesting they go back to his hotel room right now, before he left for Cincinnati, but her new persona of adventurous single woman hadn't quite settled in that much. Still, if *he* suggested it. . . .

Rex didn't suggest it. He paid the check, walked her back to Bodies, kissed her on the cheek at the front door, and promised to call her that evening. As she watched him drive away, she couldn't decide if she was disappointed or relieved.

***

Laney worked for a couple of hours after lunch, cleaning out old files, both paper and digital, and packing personal items. Greta called around two, and they arranged to get an early dinner out. After they hung up, Laney locked her office door and changed into workout clothes. She'd been neglecting her exercise routine ever since Bryce and Rex had come into her life—one more piece of evidence that juggling two men could be hazardous to a woman's health. If she spent all her time consuming food with them instead of exercising, it wouldn't be long before she'd be putting on pounds. Of course, either of them would be more than happy to help her work off the calories in a way that she was sure would be a lot more fun than a treadmill and free weights!

She worked out hard for an hour and a half, warming up on the treadmill, making her muscles scream in protest on the weight machines and free weights, and finished off with a sweat-producing spinning session. The almost unnatural burst of energy she had felt at lunch after the sudden realization that she was a free woman gave her the boost she needed to push her body to its limits. She knew she would pay for it the next day, but for now, the physical exertion felt incredibly good.

She showered, shampooed, and fluffed out her hair. By the time she dressed and applied fresh make-up, it had dried enough to be presentable. Greta stuck her head in the door as she was closing her locker.

"Hey," she said. "Ready?"

"Definitely! I need something cold to drink. Preferably with alcohol in it."

Laney dropped the bag containing her wet gym clothes off at her car, and the two of them walked to the Moonglow. It was a few minutes past five, and the happy hour crowd was starting to arrive. Laney asked the hostess for the booth that she and Rex had had earlier. It was a great booth for lunch with a sexy man, but it was also a great booth in which to share confidences with a friend.

"So how was dinner with ol' Blue Eyes last night?" Greta asked after the waitress had left with their drink orders.

"Life has gotten complicated," Laney said, sighing. "Let's look at the menus first. I've got so much to tell you that, if I start now, we'll never get our food."

When the waitress brought their drinks, they placed their food orders. As soon as she was out of earshot, Laney began filling Greta in, starting with dinner the night before, continuing to the conversation with Dee that morning, and ending with lunch. She had just finished her story when the waitress brought their food.

"Wow! You weren't kidding when you said your life has gotten complicated." Greta unwrapped her silverware and spread the cloth napkin over her lap. "You go for three years turning down men's advances and now this. You actually want both of them, don't you?"

"Is it that obvious?"

"Oh, yeah. Your eyes get this look when you talk about either one of them."

"What look?"

"You know what look. Don't play dumb with me, sweetie."

"Okay, okay." Laney cut a large piece of stuffed chicken breast, forked it and put it in her mouth. She suddenly felt starved. Sublimation, she wondered? Using food as a substitute for sex? Maybe I'd better go jogging this evening.

"Do you think I should see a doctor?" she said after she had chewed and swallowed.

"What?" Greta looked up from cutting her steak, surprised. "Why? Is there something wrong?"

"I'm wondering if there is," Laney said. "I mean, maybe I'm in early menopause or something. You know—hormones going all whacko on me."

Greta cracked up. She dropped her steak knife and fork on her plate and leaned back in the booth, laughing.

"Shhhh!" Laney leaned forward. "Hush! I'm serious."

"Oh, my God!" Greta dabbed at her eyes with her napkin, then burst into another fit of laughter.

Laney glared at her friend, but within a few moments she was smiling, and soon she was choking with laughter right along with Greta. The waitress popped her head around the corner of the booth to check on them, smiled, shook her head, and left without saying anything. Neither of them could have replied if she had.

Just before they keeled over from lack of oxygen, their laughter began to subside. They gasped and wiped their eyes with their napkins. Greta poked around in her purse and pulled out a pack of tissues. She took one and shoved the pack across the table to Laney.

"I know it's tacky to blow my nose at the table, but you'll just have to live with it." She blew hard into the tissue. "Oh, my word! You just about did me in with that hormone comment."

Laney helped herself to a tissue from the pack and blew her own nose, grateful they were in a booth where few other patrons could see them. She wondered if the people on the other side of her seat back thought the two women in the booth behind them were drunk.

"Okay, so maybe it sounds silly, but I really am kind of serious," she said. "You know this isn't like me, Greta."

"It's not like the old you," Greta said. "But maybe this is the new you."

"Well, the new me is gonna get the old me in trouble." Laney cut another piece of chicken and popped it in her mouth.

"My chicken's getting cold," she mumbled around the food.

They ate for a few minutes without talking, hurrying to get the food in while it was still warm. The waitress came by when they were almost finished.

"You ladies certainly look like you're having a good time," she said, smiling. "Can I get you anything else."

"Common sense?" Laney said. Greta chuckled.

"I won't ask you to expand on *that* comment," the waitress said. "But I bet it involves a man. Since I don't have any common sense on that account to spare, how about some dessert instead?"

Greta ordered apple pie a la mode and Laney chose a chocolate brownie smothered in fudge syrup and topped with ice cream and nuts. She usually avoided desserts, but found she craved one today. More sublimation, she guessed. She might have to give in to the sexual urges she was feeling just to keep from gaining weight. Even if it didn't work, it sounded like a good excuse.

"So what should I do?" Laney asked when the waitress had left with their order.

"Don't you mean 'who' should you do?" Greta said. "I can't answer that for you, but I'll try to help you work it out. First, what do you want from either of them—aside from hot sex, I mean?"

"I don't know that I want anything from them other than hot sex." They both chuckled. "I mean, it's not like I'm looking for a husband. Been there, done that, not sure I ever want to do it again."

"Do you want a relationship or is a one-night stand enough?"

"I don't think a one-night stand is enough. I'd need at least a week's worth."

"Will you stop!" Greta started laughing again and shook her head, holding her breath, trying to control her laughter. "You're killing me!"

"Okay, okay. I'll be serious."

Laney didn't know what was wrong with her. No wonder Greta was reacting the way she was. Greta was the girlfriend who was known for making outrageous and suggestive comments, not Laney, the serious-as-a-stroke girlfriend. It was as if the realization of her freedom had unlocked some alter ego and that creature was running amuck.

"I don't know if I want a relationship," she said. "I do think I'd like to get to know either Rex or Bryce better. Not just in that way," she added when Greta snorted. "They both seem like nice interesting men."

She leaned forward and lowered her voice.

"You know what occurred to me," she said. "I realized during lunch that I was going to have enough money and time to travel anywhere any time I wanted. I could go to Atlanta to see Rex and to California to see Bryce."

Greta's eyes widened. "You mean, carry on with both of them at the same time?"

"Well, of course, I wouldn't *really* do that. I'm just saying it occurred to me."

"Who are you and what have you done with my friend?"

Laney laughed. Just then the waitress arrived with their desserts and they dug in. After a few bites, Greta spoke.

"Carrying on affairs with both of them sounds very appealing," she said. "But it's not you, Laney. And it's asking for trouble. Sooner or later, they would both decide they wanted to come visit you at the same time. Or one would decide he wanted to take the relationship to the next level. Too many possible complications. It wouldn't end well. Rex, Bryce, and maybe you would get hurt."

Laney stared at her for a moment, while a bite of ice-cream-and-fudge-saturated brownie melted in her mouth. She swallowed and nodded.

"You're right. It wouldn't work." She sighed and leaned back against her seat. "So what do I do? Who do I pick? Rex is the more logical choice—he's the right age, he's successful and stable, but. . . ."

"But Bryce has gotten under your skin." Greta finished for her.

Laney nodded. "Yeah, he has. Way under. Last night after dinner when Rex was kissing me, I was getting all turned on by it and thinking about going up to his hotel room with him. Then I thought of Bryce."

"And you went home alone." Greta looked at her with sympathy. "I think you just answered your own question about what you should do."

"What I *should* do or what I want to do? Just because I want Bryce doesn't mean he's the best choice."

"Are you worried that he is after your money like Dee said?"

"No, no." Laney waved her hand, brushing the idea away as ridiculous. "Of course not. Even if he were, I'm not that stupid. But he's not that kind of person. At least I don't think he is."

Greta nodded. "I don't think he is either. He doesn't seem all that impressed with the things that money can buy."

"Exactly! That's just something Greg dreamed up in the hopes of turning me against Bryce. I could throttle him for having planted that in Dee's mind."

"He's needed throttling for a long time. If he'd kept his thing in his pants, he wouldn't have to worry about the California competition." Greta snorted in disgust.

"Well, at least I've got a few days to think about it," Laney said. She pushed the dessert away, half of the brownie unfinished, her desire for something sweet sated. "Bryce isn't due back until Friday, and Rex is gone until at least late tomorrow."

"Dee leaves tomorrow, too, doesn't she?"

Laney nodded.

"It's good that she'll be gone by the time Bryce gets back," Greta said. "That eliminates one obstruction."

"Never thought of my daughter as a 'obstruction' before," Laney muttered.

"The description fits this time," Greta said. "Who knows? You may spend a wild night or two with Bryce, and that will be enough to get him out of your system. If Dee were here and found out, that might cause a strain between the two of you. Right now, she's embarrassed and hurt by his rejecting her in favor of her mother. It would be shame for a one- or two-night stand to cause more problems between the two of you."

"And what if it develops into more than a one- or two-night stand?"

"Then she'll have to accept it. Just no sense in causing unnecessary problems until you know it's worth it."

"What if she doesn't accept it?"

"Dee is an intelligent young woman," Greta said. "She's you, only younger. She'll have a lot of time on her trip to get over her hurt feelings about Bryce turning her down, and she'll have time to think over what you told her about adult boundaries. If she comes home to something serious between you and Bryce, she'll be halfway to dealing with it."

"I hope you're right."

"I'm always right, sweetie. Haven't you figured that out by this time? Now, let's pay the tab and get out of here. Lee is due home tomorrow morning, and I need to shave my legs and armpits—and do some bush-hogging—so he doesn't hurt himself when he shows me how much he's missed me."

CHAPTER 12

Dee called early the following morning to say goodbye. She sounded excited about her trip, and Laney envied her just a little. She'd never done anything spontaneous like that when she was young—unless getting pregnant counted. She was glad Dee was taking advantage of her youth and freedom, while at the same time she was worried about her baby. She wondered if there was ever a point in a mother's life when that ambivalence about a child's decisions changed. Maybe by the time Dee hit menopause . . . ?

She wasn't as sore as she expected to be after her workout the day before, so after they hung up, she threw on shorts and a tee and went for a short run. It was barely six-thirty, but the day was already warming up. It was shaping up to be a scorcher—more like an August day than a June one. There wasn't any need for her to go into Bodies today. Everything was pretty much ready to be moved out of the office once the papers were signed. It might be a good day to stay inside in the air conditioning, do some housecleaning, and kick back with a good book. In other words, it might feel good to have a normal day again.

She had just finished lunch after spending the morning making her house sparkle when Greg called. When she saw who it was on the caller ID, she was tempted to let the answering machine get it. Still, it might be something about Dee or about the sale, so she picked up just before it rolled to the machine.

"Hey, there," Greg said when she answered. His voice had an intimate sound to it, low and warm, the way she remembered it had sounded back when they were young and in love. She wondered if he had rehearsed it before he dialed or if it was an unconscious thing with him. She waited for him to continue.

"Dee got off okay this morning," he said after a moment of silence.

"I know. She called me to say goodbye."

"I wish we could have seen her off together."

"We spent some time together yesterday."

"I know, but it would have been nice to have all been together on her last day."

"Greg, she's going on a trip, not dying. Is this all you called about?"

"Whoa, what's up with you? You sound like you got up on the wrong side of the bed this morning."

"I was in a good mood until you called."

"Huh? What did I do?"

"You know perfectly well what you did. Dee and I talked yesterday. She was worried about me, thanks to you."

"She told you what I figured out, huh?" Greg sounded satisfied with himself. He had known Dee would go running to Laney with his "theory." That he would use their daughter to further his own agenda made Laney dislike him even more than she already did. "I knew she was worried after we talked, but I told her I'd look into it. I didn't think she'd run straight to you."

"Oh, can the crap, Greg! You seeded her mind with your crazy ideas, because you knew damn well she'd come running to me! That was exactly what you wanted her to do! And what do you mean, you'll look into it?"

"I swear, Laney, I didn't think she'd say anything to you. At least, not until after I found out more about Adams."

"And just how do you intend to find out more about Bryce?"

"I've talked to a couple of people and got a referral for a private detective in Louisville. I have an appointment with him tomorrow morning."

"You what?" Laney gripped the handset so tightly her fingers began to cramp. She ignored them. "How dare you!"

"I dare because I love you, Laney. You know that. Adams is up to no good. I know you've been lonely the last three years, but he's blinded you with his charm. I just want to do what's right for you."

"If you wanted to do what's right for me, you'd leave me the hell alone! And you'd leave Bryce alone! He hasn't done a thing to deserve all this. Nothing has happened between us. Although . . . ," she knew it wasn't wise, but she couldn't resist, "you're doing a great job of pushing me in his direction."

"Don't say that!" Greg's tone was sharp.

"Is that an order?"

"Laney, he's after your money. He sees you as an easy mark that he can take for whatever he wants."

"You might be right that he intends to take me for whatever he wants, but I assure you what he wants isn't money."

"So you're just going to go ahead and whore around with him, is that it?" Greg couldn't hide the anger in his voice. "You don't care about embarrassing me by fooling around with a guy you used to babysit?"

"Why, Greg, here I thought you were concerned for my welfare when all the time you were worried you might be embarrassed? Did you think to mention that to our daughter when you were filling her head with your paranoid ideas?"

"Dee's embarrassed, too. How could you do something like that to your own daughter?"

"I haven't done anything," Laney said. "Yet."

"Is that a threat?"

"No, it's my way of telling you that who I want to date or sleep with or even marry is none of your damn business! And one more thing—if you keep this up, I will sign a restraining order on you. Once this sale is final, I don't ever want to set eyes on you again or talk to you again unless it involves our daughter. Do you understand?"

"You can't mean that."

"I can and do. And stay away from Bryce. I intend to tell him about your private investigator."

"Laney, please. . . ," Greg was pleading now.

"Goodbye, Greg." Laney hung up.

She sat for several minutes at the counter by the phone, unable to stop shaking from the anger that was coursing through her body. A private detective! Was Greg serious? Was he really that paranoid about Bryce that he would go to the extreme of hiring a detective to look into his background? What did he think he was going to find? A string of ex-lovers left destitute thanks to Bryce? A prison record for confidence schemes? What? Greg was starting to sound crazy, and for a second, Laney felt a little trickle of fear. She pushed it away. Greg was obviously nuts, but he wasn't violent.

She had cleaned everything but her windows. They needed it, but before lunch, she'd decided she'd done enough housework for the day. Now the mindless exertion was exactly what she needed to work out her anger. Two hours later, the windows sparkled and her equilibrium was restored. She fixed a cup of green tea, downloaded a book she'd been meaning to read, settled back on the couch with her Kindle, and put the men in her life out of her mind.

***

She slept late Thursday morning, crawling out of bed at eight-thirty. She started the coffeemaker and plugged her phone back in. She'd unplugged it after the conversation with Greg, knowing he'd be likely to call her again at some point during the day to see if she'd calmed down. She'd turned her cell off as well. When she powered it up, she saw she had five messages waiting. Three were Greg, but the other two numbers were unfamiliar. She hit Listen and waited while the phone connected with her voice mail.

The first message was from Greg. He'd called back less than thirty minutes after they'd talked.

"Um, Laney, I forgot to tell you when we talked— Larry called. The closing is set for next Friday at one. If that's not good for you, let me know as soon as possible." A moment of silence, then, "Love you."

Thank God, Laney thought, feeling relief wash through her. Just one more week and I won't have to have anything to do with him ever again. There was still Dee, of course. They'd have to attend her college graduation, and one day there would be a wedding and grandchildren, but maybe by then Greg would have found someone and moved on.

The next message was from Rex. Laney had forgotten he'd promised to call. The service gave the time as five-thirty the previous evening.

"Hello, beautiful. Sorry I missed you. And I'm even sorrier that I won't be making it back today like I thought. We had a bad fire at one of our Iowa malls, and I need to run up there. I'm at the Cincinnati airport now. I'm not sure how long I'll be gone, but I should be back mid-week at the latest."

In time for the closing, Laney wondered?

The next two messages were from Greg, the first at six-thirty, followed by another a little over an hour later. He sounded like he'd been drinking when he made the first one and it was even more noticeable on the second. He started out begging her forgiveness, telling her he loved her and was so sorry for everything he'd done wrong, then moved on to how worried he was about her, building up to what a scoundrel "that Adams asshole" was. He ended by promising that she'd thank him in the long run.

That last comment sounded like he hadn't given up on the idea of hiring a private detective. Well, let him waste his money! Bryce had nothing to hide, and if Greg went so far as to pay to have someone follow Bryce, he might not like what he saw. Still, she would warn Bryce when he returned that his privacy was about to be invaded.

She was surprised when she played the last message. It was Bryce. The time on the message was ten-thirty, about the time she'd been getting ready for bed.

"It's me." She felt a little tingle at the sound of his voice, a tingle she realized had been missing when she'd listened to Rex's message. "I'm back. It's late and you're not answering your phone, so I'm not going to bother you tonight. I want to see you tomorrow to explain about Dee." After a second of silence, the call disconnected.

She hurried to the window and looked out. Bryce's rental stood in the drive, but his curtains were still drawn. He was probably still asleep. She took a few minutes to brush her teeth, comb her hair, and throw on a pair of jeans and a tee. She tucked an item from the top of her dresser into the back pocket of her jeans and went out, locking her door behind her. With any luck, she might be gone a while.

She knocked hard on his front door, waited a minute that seemed to drag on for hours, and knocked again. A few seconds later, the door opened. A sense of déjà vu washed over her as she saw the same unruly hair, half-zipped jeans, and shirtless chest she'd been treated to a week earlier. Was that all the longer it had been, she thought with amazement? Only one week?

His eyes widened when he saw her, and he smiled that adorable crooked smile. "Well. Good morning," he said.

"Hey," she said. "I wanted to come over right away. I need to apologize for how I talked to you Sunday night. Dee told me everything. I'm sorry I jumped to the wrong conclusion and I just want to say. . . ."

He took her hand and pulled her into the house, slamming the door and pressing her up against it, his body against hers. His mouth closed on hers, cutting off the rest of her apology. His hands slid over her back to her buttocks, pulling her hips forward against the growing bulge in his jeans. She groaned and pressed herself tighter against him, kissing his lips, his eyes, his neck, his lips again.

They half-walked, half-stumbled to the couch sitting against the wall opposite the door. He collapsed back onto it in a sitting position and pulled her onto his lap, her legs on either side of his thighs as they had been in the front seat of his car Sunday night. She grabbed hold of his hair and lowered her mouth to his. The world around them disappeared for her, all of her senses focused on only Bryce. He tasted of toothpaste, clean and sweet, and she ran her tongue around the inside of his mouth and his tongue, reveling in the taste of him. She felt his sweat against her forearms where they rested on his neck and the silkiness of his hair wrapped around her fingers, and she breathed deeply of his wonderful smell, a mixture of soap and shampoo and man. Her ears were filled only with his ragged breathing and his groans, leaving no room for any sounds from outside.

His hands moved over her body, as if he were a blind man trying to form a picture of her by touch alone. When they slid under her tee, she stopped kissing him long enough to raise her arms so he could slide the shirt over her head. He made an unintelligible sound that she took to be appreciation of the fact that she hadn't bothered with a bra when she'd dressed. She bent to kiss him, but before she could claim his lips, he pressed them to her right nipple and began teasing it with his tongue, then sucking long and hard, then moved to the left nipple and lightly licking again. Her breasts had never been particularly sensitive before, but when his mouth touched them, they seemed to catch fire. She wrapped her fingers in his hair and pressed his face against them, wanting it to go on forever.

When they could stand it no longer, she stood and slipped out of her jeans. He raised his hips from the couch and slid his over his bare feet. She stood for a moment, simply looking at the beautiful man before her, from his unruly hair and beautiful eyes, down across his wide tan chest with its sprinkling of curly brown hair to his manhood, standing at full attention, glowing in its whiteness against the tan of his thighs and abdomen. His eyes were performing their own appraisal of her, his gaze moving over her body in a way that was almost tactile. That it was obvious he liked what he saw made her feel powerful, and she moved forward to claim him. He started to reach for her, but stopped.

"I'll be right back." He started to stand, but she pushed him back down. Reaching into the back pocket of the jeans she still held in her hand, she withdrew the foil-wrapped package she had purchased on her way home the evening before. She held it out to him. He took it, smiled that crooked smile, and pulled her onto his lap.

"It looks like you came over here to seduce me," he murmured, as he nuzzled her neck. He had his arms around her, and she heard the sound of the foil packet being torn open.

"I thought I might get lucky."

"I'm the lucky one." He moved his hands between them, and she rose onto her knees, kissing him hard and deep while he slid the condom on. Then he took her hips and pulled her down. He slid into her and she gasped with the pleasure of it.

As they moved together, he held her gaze with his own, staring into her eyes as if he were looking into her soul, his lips slightly parted. She yearned to kiss those lips, but she wanted to look at him more, to watch as he struggled to hold back his orgasm, trying to prolong the pleasure for both of them. As wave after wave of sensation rolled through her, building in intensity each time she moved on him, she looked into those eyes and knew she'd never get enough of this man.

He put up a valiant fight, but the little tic that started at the corner of his beautiful mouth and the almost pained look that came into his eyes told her he was losing the battle. She pulled his mouth to her then and kissed him long and deep, groaning as she surrendered moments before he did, shuddering uncontrollably with the release. They clung to each other, mouths pressed together, until he began to soften. Then he rolled with her, laying her gently down on her back on the couch. She looked at him lying on his side pressed between her and the back of the couch, and laughed softly.

"What?" he said, running the tips of the fingers of his left hand gently across the side of her face, brushing back her hair.

"I was just thinking that the couch your grandparents used to have sat in this very same spot. I used to read your stories to you here."

He laughed. "I loved cuddling with you then, but I gotta say, this beats that."

They snuggled together for a few minutes, not talking, before he pushed himself up from the couch.

"Be right back," he said.

Laney sighed, enjoying the rear view as he walked out of the room. He looked like a living statue, a sculpture of male perfection, with his broad muscular back, rounded buttocks, and strong legs. Laney thought she had never seen anything more beautiful, and she had never felt more content than she did at this moment. She closed her eyes, savoring the feeling, refusing to let herself think about the complications that might wait outside these walls.

She heard him come back and opened her eyes. He took her hand and pulled her up from the couch.

"Let's go cuddle somewhere with more room," he said and led her to his bedroom.

Two hours later, the need for food drove them from the bed to the kitchen. Bryce had slipped his jeans back on and padded around the kitchen in his bare feet, gathering what he needed to prepare breakfast. Laney wore only her panties and one of his tees. She poured water into the coffeemaker and scooped coffee into the filter, all the while steadying herself by holding onto the counter. She didn't trust her legs to support her.

"Whatsa' matter?" Bryce came up behind her and wrapped his arms around her, burying his face in her neck. "You look a little wobbly."

"I *feel* a little wobbly." She leaned into him, loving the feel of his strong arms around her.

"Are you complaining?" He nibbled at her neck, tickling her. She squirmed and twisted around to face him.

"No! I'm not complaining at all!"

"Ah! I see. You're bragging."

"Maybe I am." She pulled his lips to her own and kissed him long and hard. She felt him starting to grow and felt herself start to respond, and pulled back, looking at him in wonder. "My God, what are you doing to me? I can't get enough of you."

"Good." He moved to kiss her again, but she put a hand on his chest, stopping him.

"Food," she croaked, as if she were a dying woman. "I need food."

He laughed, gave her a quick peck and released her.

"Omelets, coming right up," he said, adjusting his jeans as he turned to the stove.

"Be careful around the hot stove with that," she said, running her hand lightly over the bulge. "I wouldn't want you to burn it, although I suppose if you did, I could kiss it and make it all better."

"Keep talking like *that* and you'll have to wait for lunch."

"Okay, okay, I'll behave." She raised her hands in mock surrender.

She poured a cup of coffee for him and one for herself. She sat on one of the stools at the breakfast bar, sipping her coffee and watching him cook. He chopped onions, green peppers, and ham, mixing the ingredients into the beaten eggs with the practiced ease of someone well acquainted with a kitchen. While the omelets cooked, he pulled a bowl of strawberries, another of chopped melon, and a bunch of red grapes from the fridge, and scooped some of each into individual serving bowls. She watched in awe as he successfully flipped the omelets, something she'd never been able to master. While the omelet finished cooking, he toasted two English muffins. He slid the omelets onto plates, placed the muffins and fruit bowls beside them, and carried both to the bar. After gathering up silverware, napkins, butter, and jam, he returned and pulled out a stool of his own.

"More coffee?" he asked before sitting down.

She nodded, and he topped off their cups before sitting down.

"Wow!" she said.

He looked up from his plate. "Hmmm?"

"All this." She waved her hand at the food. "I mean—will you marry me?"

She said it jokingly, but he didn't smile.

"Gladly," he said, his voice soft.

They stared at each other for several seconds, the food forgotten. Then he smiled.

"Mom taught me all this. Said she wanted to make sure I'd make some woman a good wife one day."

Laney laughed, relieved. He had looked so serious—but that was ridiculous, wasn't it? Probably one of those things a man does to keep a woman interested. Tease her with suggestions of commitment—the reverse of a woman playing hard to get to keep a man interested. Oh, the games people play!

"I almost forgot," she said when they were halfway through the meal. "Greg is on the warpath."

Bryce smiled that crooked smile. Damn, it was so sexy!

"Is he now?" he said.

Laney started to tell him Greg thought he was after her money, but stopped. For one thing, she didn't want to make a big deal about the money she was about to get, but more than that, she didn't want to insult him. Once Greg's suspicions were aired between them, Bryce would always be wondering if she was just a little suspicious herself. There's no way to defend yourself against something like that, and it would be always be there, hanging over whatever might develop between them.

"He told me he's hiring a private detective to look into your background," she said, deciding to leave it at that.

"A private detective! Seriously?" Bryce leaned back, his food forgotten.

"Seriously. He's taken a major disliking to you."

"Well, I can understand that. I wouldn't like me either if I were in his shoes, but a private detective? What does he think he's going to find out?"

"Who knows? He's crazy. I just wanted to warn you."

Bryce shrugged. "Let him waste his money. He'll find out I'm the poster boy for the All-American guy. Honest, brave, and loyal."

"And full of himself." Laney laughed.

"Remind me to check and make sure there are no gaps in the bedroom curtains." That smile again. "If the P.I. got a picture—well, I'd order an 8x10, but it would probably put your ex six feet under."

"Hush!" Laney laughed, blushing as she envisioned the picture in her mind.

They finished their breakfast quickly. She could tell from the way Bryce kept shifting on the stool that his jeans were starting to feel just a little snug, and she was anxious to help him take care of the problem. It was the neighborly thing to do, after all.

CHAPTER 13

By the time Laney returned to her house Friday morning, she wasn't sure she'd ever be able to sit down again. She had lost count of how many times they'd made love, but she was grateful to the Boy Scouts for teaching Bryce to be prepared. He'd also made a stop at a drugstore Wednesday evening, but he'd had the foresight to buy a really large box of condoms. She had only bought a three-pack and had only taken one of those with her when she went next door. Oh, well, she thought. I'm new at this. I'll learn.

She had begged off more lovemaking when she learned Bryce was expecting workmen later that morning. He had decided to replace his grandparents' carpet with tile everywhere in the house except the bedrooms. When she started to dress, he grabbed her hand and said they had at least half an hour before the installers arrived. She'd laughed and pulled away, knowing if she didn't go home, they'd probably still be at it when the workers arrived.

She supposed Bryce's youth had something to do with his stamina, but Greg had never been like that, not even when they were first engaged. Twice a night occasionally, but that was about it. And it wasn't just Bryce's repeated encore performances that were different. The man had style—penis, mouth, hands, eyes, and words—he used it all to bring her pleasure. She had never felt so special and so loved and so desired.

My God, she thought. I hope he's not after my money. I'd probably give him every dime and consider it money well spent! She was still chuckling as she got in the shower.

Bryce had to stay around the house all day while the tile installers were there, but they'd arranged to meet for dinner that evening. Her house was clean thanks to her marathon bout with housework Wednesday, so nothing to kill time with there. Surprised she had the energy to even think of it, she decided a workout at Bodies was in order. After next Friday she would have to buy a membership like everybody else, so she might as well take advantage of being an owner while she could. And maybe Starbucks with Greta—she picked up the phone and gave her a call.

"So what's up?" Greta said as they settled at a table at Starbucks. "Have you made a decision yet about which hunk you're going to hop in bed with? Or has Rex made the first cut because he's in town and Bryce isn't?"

"Actually Rex isn't in town. There was a fire at an Iowa mall he and his partners own, and he had to run up there for a few days."

"Ah, so little Brycie has a chance after all!" Greta nodded. "Good! I'm rooting for the boy. He's due back today, right? Got your apology all worked out?"

Laney smiled. "Been there, done that."

"Huh?"

"Bryce got home Wednesday night—although I didn't know it until yesterday morning when I listened to the message he left me. You might say we've worked out our misunderstanding."

"Oh, my God! Tell me!"

"All I'm going to say is, he accepted my apology. In fact, he accepted it many, many times between yesterday morning and this morning."

Laney couldn't help but laugh out loud at the expression on Greta's face. Her latte and Danish forgotten, Greta sat with a stunned look on her face, mouth open, and eyes wide. She finally snapped her mouth shut and blinked.

"Really?"

"Really." Laney shook her head. "He's . . . I can't even put into words all that he is, Greta. I just know I'm happy. I may never be able to wear tight jeans again, but I'm happy."

"Oh, my Lord! He worked you over good, huh? Remember, I said I wanted details."

"Well, I'm not giving them to you. Let's just say Bryce knows what he's doing." Laney's smile disappeared. "It's not just that. He makes me feel— well, he makes me feel loved. And valued, like I'm the most important thing in the world to him. Do you know what I mean?"

"Yes," Greta said. "I do. I'm lucky to have a husband who still makes me feel that way. You want to know what I think?"

"Whether I do or not, I'm sure you're going to tell me." Laney smiled.

"You're falling in love with the guy."

Laney stared at her for a moment. Was that what was happening? Was she in love with Bryce, or was it just the afterglow from the most amazing sex she'd ever experienced? How did a woman separate the two anyway and keep from making a mistake that could screw up the rest of her life?

"I don't know," she said. "I mean, yes, I guess I do 'feel' like I am, but does that make it a good idea or even make it real? An amazing twenty-four hours with a man doesn't mean he's the right choice for the long term, does it?"

"Of course not. But the fact you're even wondering if he's the right choice for the long term tells me you care a lot about him."

"Or maybe it's just proof that I'm not very experienced when it comes to men."

"And it could be that," Greta admitted. "Time will tell. Don't analyze it to death. Just go with the flow and don't make any rash decisions. It will work out, or it won't."

Laney laughed. "How did you get to be so wise?"

"Born that way. So, when do you see him again?"

"We're going to dinner tonight. He's got people installing tile in his house today so he had to stick around for that."

"Good thing. Sounds like your bod needed a break. What are you going to do about Rex?"

"Well, I'm certainly not going to see both of them!" Laney said. "Even if I was mentally and emotionally equipped for the job, the last twenty-four hours taught me that I'm not physically equipped! When he calls, I'll tell him I won't be seeing him anymore."

"I think that's a wise decision." Greta gobbled the last bite of her Danish, wiped her fingers with her napkin, and stood. " Now, let's go work off these calories. Although, based on what you just told me, I doubt you need to."

***

It was the same booth at the Moonglow again. Laney blushed a little when the hostess escorted them to the private booth she had shared with Rex and later Greta. Maybe I should use my fingernail file to scratch my initials in the tabletop, she thought.

Bryce was wearing khakis, pressed and creased, and a white button-down shirt open at the collar. It was the first time she'd seen him in anything other than jeans or swim trunks. She'd suspected he didn't own any other clothes and was relieved to see she was wrong. The clothes—even if they were just business casual—made him seem less boyish and made her feel less uncomfortable about being seen with a younger man.

"So how much did the installers get done today?" she asked after they'd placed their drink orders.

"Kitchen and bath. It has to set up at least overnight. They'll be back tomorrow to grout those two rooms. They do the living room and hall next week."

"What time are they coming tomorrow?"

"Afraid they'll interrupt something?" That adorable crooked smile again! Laney felt herself go from zero to ready at the sight of it!

"How did you know?"

"That look in your eyes gives you away—and it turns me on." His voice dropped, the menu in his hands forgotten. "I could do you right here in the booth."

She slipped her foot out of her shoe and slid it between his legs. Her toes began to massage the bulge in his crotch. His eyes widened and he let his breath out in a whoosh.

"Here you go." The waiter placed the glass of wine in front of her. It was the only drawback to the booth, she decided. It was so private the wait staff could sneak up on a woman before she knew it. She kept her foot in place and Bryce moved his menu over his lap to block it from view, a thin film of sweat beginning to glisten on his forehead.

"Are you ready to order or do you need a few more minutes?"

"Uh—a few more minutes, thanks." Bryce shifted in his seat and pretended to be reading the menu.

"You're killing me!" He whispered as soon as the waiter had walked away.

"You don't like it?" Laney gave him one last toe rub and pulled her foot back. He gave a little groan, and she smiled in satisfaction. "We'll save it for later then."

She was a little surprised at herself. She'd never done anything spontaneous like that and in a public place with Greg, but then Greg wasn't a man who inspired that sort of thing. Or maybe that wasn't fair. They had been little more than kids when they met, both afflicted with the self-consciousness of the young. The back seat of his car on whatever lovers lane was popular at the moment was as adventuresome as they got—not to mention they could only afford dinner at MickeyD's. Fast food booths hardly lent themselves to toe jobs.

"Maybe we could order food to go?"

She laughed. "Nope. We're going to enjoy a nice meal right here. Dessert will wait."

"I don't know if I can," Bryce grumbled.

When they finished their meal and the waiter had taken Bryce's credit card, Bryce took her hand. "Let's go away for the weekend," he said.

"Go away? Where?"

"We could run up to Cincinnati. Get a nice hotel, maybe see a play, walk along the river."

Laney's first reaction was to think of reasons she couldn't go—the club, Dee, things she needed to do, then remembered that none of those things were valid excuses anymore. She smiled, that sense of freedom she had first experienced in this same booth with Rex flooding through her again.

"Let's do it," she said. "When?"

"After I let the tile guys in tomorrow. It's only a ninety-minute drive. We'll have all day Saturday and can come back late Sunday."

"Don't you have to be home while the installers are there?"

"I'm not gonna worry about it. They seem like nice guys and they're bonded. If they abscond with my grandma's couch and TV, it won't be the end of the world." He kissed her hand and released it. "I'd let them have a shot at the family jewels to have a weekend away with you."

"Smooth talker."

Bryce signed the tab and replaced his card in his wallet. They had just exited the restaurant when Laney's cell rang. Checking the screen, she saw it was Rex. She hesitated a moment, then hit Ignore and dropped the phone back into her purse. She looked up to see Bryce looking at her questioningly.

"You could have answered that, you know," he said. "I'm not your crazy jealous ex."

"It's nothing like that." She started to tell him the call was from Greta, and she could call her later, but stopped. Lying was no way to start a relationship and that was what this was, wasn't it? The start of a relationship? "Okay, yes, it was. That was Rex."

"Ah." Bryce grinned that crooked grin, nodding his head. "Taylor is as persistent as I am, I see."

"Earlier in the week—when I was still upset with you, I went to dinner with Rex. He had to go out of town after that. There was a fire at a mall he and his partners own. He's called a few times. That's all."

"I swear I didn't set the fire to get rid of the competition, although if I'd thought of it. . . ."

Bryce grinned and Laney laughed. He pulled her to him and kissed her long and hard. The driver of a passing car honked his horn and yelled, "Get a room!"

"He's got the right idea," Bryce said.

He pulled back, but left his arm around her as they walked to the car. Laney snuggled against him, her arm around his waist, suddenly not caring who saw them. In fact, she realized with surprise, she wanted to be seen with him. She wanted the world to know that this handsome, sexy—and, yes, young—man was with her. Greta was right. She was falling in love with the man she used to babysit.

***

The next morning while Bryce let the installers in and instructed them on locking up after they were done, Laney went next door and threw some clothes in a suitcase. As usual, she packed more than she could wear, but she didn't know what she might need. She guessed they'd keep it casual, but Bryce had mentioned a play so she made sure to take a casual summer dress and low heels. She had just finished when he knocked on the door. When she opened it, she already had her suitcase and house keys in hand, knowing if she let him inside, they might never make it to Cincinnati.

They talked and laughed on their way north, discovering they had similar taste in music as they station-surfed on the radio. Laney couldn't help but compare this drive to the one they'd taken last Saturday. Then she had been the sensible older woman and old family friend showing the younger man around the area while trying to ignore how attractive he was; now she was his lover. The tension from a week ago was gone, replaced by a comfortable anticipation. They didn't drive more than half a mile without touching— her hand on his thigh, his hand brushing her hair back from her face, her head on his shoulder. It was as if they had to constantly reassure themselves that the other person was real and not a dream.

The night before had been as amazing as Thursday had been. They hadn't made love as often, not because they didn't want to, but because Laney was still recovering from the marathon sex of the day before. After returning to Bryce's from the restaurant, they had cuddled on the couch, watched late movies, sipped wine, and kissed. A lot. Those kisses eventually led to gentle lovemaking in the bed before they drifted off to sleep, something they hadn't gotten enough of the night before. Bryce had set the alarm and it went off at eight. The installers weren't due until nine-thirty—plenty of time for another round of slow and easy lovemaking, coffee, and a quick bagel with cream cheese.

They crossed over the Ohio River just before eleven-thirty. Laney had assumed they'd pick a hotel at random and stop to get a room, so she was surprised when Bryce drove into downtown and pulled up at valet parking for the 21c Museum Hotel. Laney had heard about the hotel that was next door to the Contemporary Arts Center and was itself a museum for contemporary art, but she'd never been there and hadn't expected Bryce to even know about it.

"Are you sure we can get in here?" she said. "They're probably full. And expensive."

"I called ahead. We have a reservation."

Well, well, she thought, as she accompanied Bryce into the hotel and across the lobby to the check-in desk. He seemed completely at home in the luxurious lobby, surrounded by paintings and sculptures. Guess this man isn't all jeans and T-shirts after all. He seemed more at ease than she was.

She was even more surprised when he escorted her into a suite that was nearly half the size of her house. The seating area with its sectional sofa was almost as large as her living room and the bathroom was bigger. The king size bed in the bedroom was lush and inviting.

"Bryce, this is too much!" she said. She was thrilled with the accommodations, but she didn't want him maxing out his credit card.

"Well, I did consider just getting a room instead of a suite." He grinned that adorable crooked grin. "Figured we'd spend most of our time in bed anyway. But then I remembered how much fun the couch at my house was."

He pulled her to him and kissed her long and hard, his hands moving down over her back to cup her buttocks. She clung to him, wanting him inside her more than she could remember ever wanting anything in her life. After a few minutes, they found out the couch at 21c was every bit as much fun as the one at his house.

***

Bryce wanted to get in the shower with her, but Laney pushed him back when he tried to follow her into the bathroom. "I'm hungry and I'll never get food if you're in here with me."

She locked the door and took a quick shower, smiling as she soaped all the places that were still tingling. While he showered, she dressed and put on light makeup. The hotel's restaurant, the Metropole, wasn't open for lunch on weekends, so on the recommendation of the front desk clerk, they walked a few doors up to a cozy pub with dark woodwork and comfortable booths. Bryce ordered a Cuban sandwich and Laney ordered a Reuben, both of them laughing about how the sandwiches rhymed. The waiter smiled indulgently at their silliness.

After lunch, they walked around downtown. They stopped for a few minutes on Fountain Square where a country band had attracted a group of fans. It was a perfect summer day, warm with a breeze that kept it from being too hot, music and happy people, and the smells of food of every imaginable kind wafting from restaurants and stands. They stood near the back of the crowd, Bryce behind her and slightly to the side, his arms around her waist. She leaned into him, reveling in the feel of his body against hers, knowing that it wasn't the sunshine or the music that made her see the day as perfect. It was being here with him.

They continued their walk toward the river, stopping at the Freedom Center per Laney's request and the Reds Hall of Fame per Bryce's. By the time they got to Riverfront Park, Laney's feet were starting to complain. They found an unoccupied bench with a view of the Ohio River and rested, Bryce's arm around her shoulders, his other hand holding hers. After a few moments, he kissed her on the forehead.

"Thank you," he said, his voice low and caressing.

"For what?"

"Coming with me this weekend, moving back into your old house so I could find you again, screwing my brains out."

Laney laughed and nuzzled closer.

"No thanks necessary, especially for that last one. It's been my pleasure."

"What do you say we get a cab back to the hotel? I know you're probably really, really tired from all this walking, and I bet your whole body aches. I should probably give you a full-body massage."

"Ummm—I think you're right."

They found a cab outside the park and were back in their room within fifteen minutes. Bryce had barely shut the door behind them when Laney slid her arms around his waist, pressed her body against his, and lifted her face for his kiss. He pushed her back.

"Body massage, remember?" The look in his eyes told her it wasn't easy to push her away. He removed her clothing, one article at a time, and led her to the bed.

"Face down," he commanded and she complied.

He went into the bathroom and came back out with a bottle of oil that he must have had in his Dopp kit. He set it on the nightstand while he removed his own clothing. Laney felt the bed give as he straddled her, his already hard penis resting on her buttocks. A few seconds later, she felt a trickle of oil on her back and his hands began their massage. She groaned with pleasure as his fingers probed and stroked, finding knots in her shoulders and back that she wasn't aware she had, working them until they relaxed, then moving on to the next one. He caressed her upper arms with long firm strokes, leaning with the forward motion, his penis moving against her buttocks as he did so, his breathing labored. Laney knew he was exerting every ounce of willpower he had to keep from entering her, just as she was using every ounce of willpower she had to keep herself from begging him to do it.

Suddenly she felt him shift position and a small whimper left her as she felt his penis move away from her. His hands moved down across her back and began to knead her buttocks. She groaned with pleasure. Just when she thought it couldn't get any better, she felt his tongue lightly tracing the contours of her bottom. His mouth moved to her side and she felt his hands guiding her to turn over. She twisted his hair around her fingers, holding on as if her life depended on it as his tongue began to work her clitoris, his hands still cupping her buttocks, raising her to his face.

It didn't take long. She tried unsuccessfully to mute the scream that escaped her and hoped the walls of the hotel were soundproof. She barely registered the sound of the foil packet being ripped open and the spasms were still rocking her body as he entered her, all restraint gone with hard thrusts that she returned with her own. He moaned as he reached climax, continuing to thrust hard into her, until finally he collapsed against her, still shuddering.

She wrapped her arms around him and held him close, loving the feel of his weight on top of her. His face was turned to the side and she nuzzled hers into his silky hair. They lay like that, not speaking, their breathing slowly returning to normal. After several minutes he raised up on his elbows and looked at her. Her breathing nearly stopped when she saw the tender and loving look in his eyes, and she felt her own eyes began to moisten with tears of happiness.

"I guess you know I'm crazy about you," he said.

"I . . . ," she started, but he put a finger to her lips.

"Shhhh. Not necessary to say anything. I just felt like saying it." He smiled that adorable crooked grin and she felt herself smiling in response. "You know how ducklings imprint on the first animal they see after hatching and think that's their mother? I think I imprinted on you when I was four years old."

"So you look at me as your mother?"

He laughed. "Well, okay, the comparison isn't exact. You get the idea, though. You ruined me for any other woman." He nuzzled her neck. "Or maybe I just had amazingly good taste in women even at the age of four."

"You really are a silver-tongued devil, aren't you?" Laney kissed him. "You smoothie!"

He gently brushed her hair back from her face, his expression turning serious. "Yeah, that's me," he said, his voice almost a whisper. "A smoothie who's crazy about you."

They stared at each other for a few moments before he pulled away from her and stood up. "I better get rid of this love balloon before it falls off."

"There goes that silver tongue again."

He laughed and headed for the bathroom. Laney stretched, feeling so contented and satisfied that, had she been a cat, she would have purred. Life had just gotten complicated thanks to the man in the bathroom, and maybe she would be sorry when they got back home to *real* life, but she would worry about that when the time came. For now, she wanted nothing more than to be held and kissed by Bryce, to feel him inside of her, to have him look at her the way he had when he told her he was crazy about her. If he hadn't stopped her, she would have told him she felt the same way.

"So where do you want to go for dinner?" Bryce said, coming out of the bathroom. He was still naked and she felt a rush of desire that shocked her coming so soon after the orgasm she had just had.

"Uh . . . I don't know. Where do you want to go?"

"The Metropole downstairs is open for dinner. Want to try it?"

"That's fine," she said.

Laney's cell rang just after they had placed their drink orders. A glance at the screen told her it was Greg. She pressed Ignore to silence the ring.

"Greg," she said, returning to the menu she'd been perusing. "The last person I want to talk to this evening. Or ever, for that matter."

"Little hard to do when you have a child together."

"True. But Dee's an adult now, so it's not like we have to arrange visitation or attend parent/teacher conferences together. Once this sale is final, I can be rid of him."

"He's not going to handle you and I being together very well."

Bryce delivered the comment in an offhand way, his attention focused on his menu. Laney's menu was forgotten as she looked at him, the word "together" having wiped all thoughts of food from her mind. Were they truly together? Was this more than just a heady fling, an amazing escape from the routine of their lives? He would complete the work on his grandparents' home and return to California. What then? Would they make the occasional visit to one another, the time between visits gradually growing longer and longer until one or the other of them found someone else? Or would this affair end the minute he packed up and went home?

Her phone rang again; the screen showed it was Greg.

"Speak of the devil," she said, starting to worry. "Maybe I should answer this. It might be about Dee."

Bryce nodded.

"Hello?" Laney said, just as the waiter delivered their drinks. In a low voice, Bryce told him they needed a few more minutes with the menus.

"Where the hell are you?" Greg said. He sounded angry.

"What do you want, Greg? Is Dee okay?"

"Dee? Why wouldn't she be okay?"

"You called me twice in less than five minutes. I was afraid something was wrong."

"It's not Dee. Where are you? Are you with that son-of-a-bitch Adams?"

"Hanging up now, Greg. Do not call me again."

She disconnected and hesitated for a moment before turning off her phone.

"He's on the warpath," she said. "He wanted to know if I was with you."

"Maybe you should have told him you were."

Laney shook her head. "Not while he's like this. Besides, I don't want to deal with him tonight or any time this weekend."

She opened her menu again.

"Now what do I want to eat?"

During dinner, Bryce suggested they catch a cab to the Horseshoe Casino. Laney had heard a lot about it after Greta and Lee had spent a weekend there, but she'd never been. For that matter, she'd never been in any casino. She'd been living the life of a suburban mom, wife, and business owner—a tame and boring existence that didn't have room for spontaneous trips to gambling casinos in the company of a sexy younger man. Deciding she liked the new direction her life was taking, she readily agreed.

They got a cab in front of the hotel and cuddled together in the back seat on the short ride to the Horseshoe. As they walked through the front doors, the noise—a mixture of music, voices, and the *chi-ching* of the slots assaulted them. Slot machines stretched as far as she could see across the dark brown carpet imprinted with beige horseshoes, most of the machines occupied this Saturday night by people transfixed by the spinning cylinders and their dreams. It could have been a scene from a science fiction movie where humans were plugged into machines and used as a power source for their alien overlords. Brown, bright, noisy, and creepy—those four adjectives summed up Laney's first impression of her first casino. She decided she hadn't been missing anything after all.

Or maybe she was just getting old.

She felt Bryce's hand against the small of her back as he guided her through the banks of slots. Just when she thought there was no end to them, they emerged into an area occupied by blackjack tables, poker tables, and roulette wheels on the right. The slot machines continued on the left, their sheer number indicating they were the casino's most popular draw. Laney supposed it made sense. The games of poker and blackjack required some skill and had rules to learn while slots—and roulette—were simple games of chance, no more complicated than buying lottery tickets.

"You want to play anything?" Bryce asked.

Laney shook her head. "I don't think so. But go ahead if you want to."

"Not really my thing either. Let's find a lounge and get a drink while we watch other people lose their money."

The Rock Bar and Lounge had a good crowd, but they managed to snag a couple of empty stools at the bar. The female DJ kept the dance floor full with upbeat music, the volume blocking most attempts at conversation. Laney and Bryce sipped their drinks and watched the dancers, content to communicate by touch and look.

They were halfway through their drinks when the DJ took a break. She stopped at the end of the bar where the waitresses picked up their orders and asked for something. The bartender gave her a tall glass of clear liquid garnished with a slice of lemon and another of lime.

"Be right back," Bryce said.

He hurried to the end of the bar, catching up with the DJ just as she started toward a door marked

"Employees Only." Laney saw the woman's posture straighten as she got a good look at Bryce, her breasts thrusting out, her head tilting to the side the way women sometimes do when they're being flirtatious. Forget about it, Laney thought, feeling a surprising pang of jealousy. He's mine.

Bryce seemed oblivious to his effect on the DJ. He said something to her and she glanced Laney's way, staring at her for a few seconds in a manner Laney could only describe as "appraising." Then, she shrugged and nodded. Bryce slipped something into her hand. She glanced at it and looked back at him, surprise evident on her face. She said something and nodded enthusiastically. As he made his way back to his stool, the woman watched him go, then turned and went through the employees' door.

"What was that about?" Laney asked.

"Just made a request. I wasn't sure she'd take it—most DJs in clubs don't, but thought I'd ask."

"What's the song?"

"Just a song I like." Bryce nodded at her drink. "Another?"

"Why not?" After Bryce had gotten the bartender's attention and placed their orders, she said, "So—do you gamble much?"

He shook his head. "Nope. At least, not until I opened my grandma's front door and saw you."

There was that adorable crooked grin again. Laney felt an overwhelming urge to kiss it, so she did.

"Did anyone ever tell you that you have the sexiest grin ever?" she said, sitting back down on her stool.

"I do?" He looked surprised.

"You do," she said. "Along with several other sexy features, of course."

"Maybe you'll point them out to me later."

"Maybe I will."

They grinned at each other. The sexual tension was there, Laney thought, but now that they'd already experienced one another's bodies, it was different. It was the tension of anticipation, all the back-and-forth of the pros and cons of doing anything about it gone. They'd stepped over the line, loved it, and would step over it again every chance they got, consequences be damned.

"Anyway," she said, dragging the word out like Dee was prone to do. "I just thought since you wanted to come here tonight that maybe you enjoyed gambling. Where you live, you're not that far from Las Vegas, are you?"

"San Diego is a good six- to seven-hour drive from Vegas," he said. "But there's no need to go there. Less than an hour outside of town, there are several casinos on reservation land. And there are poker parlors in San Diego and in the surrounding counties. I went a few times to the casinos and the parlors with friends back in college, but I haven't been in years."

"So you suggested coming here tonight because I look like a gambler?" Laney feigned indignation and Bryce laughed.

"Yeah, you look like the wild type who'd bet the farm on a roll of the dice," he said. "I figured I'd get you loosened up with booze and games of chance, and maybe I'd get lucky."

"Seems like sound reasoning to me."

The bartender had just delivered their second round when the DJ returned to the stage. Another few minutes passed while the DJ looked through her tracks, then she turned on the microphone.

"I don't usually take requests," she said, "but I've made an exception for the hot guy at the bar with the lucky lady. It's their anniversary and he begged me to play 'their' song, so this is for Bryce and Laney."

As *Do That To Me One More Time* began to play, Bryce took Laney's hand and led her to the dance floor to a spattering of applause. The DJ gave a thumbs-up to the surprised Laney and fanned herself with a napkin.

"You are one lucky lady," she said, "and if you have any sense, you'll do it to that hot hubby of yours more than one more time."

Bryce pulled her close, wrapping both his arms around her waist, his hands resting just below her waist where her buttocks began to curve outward. No one knew them here and Laney felt a sudden sense of abandon. She put her arms around his shoulders and pressed against him, her nipples rubbing against his hard chest, her groin caressing the bulge in his pants.

"Our anniversary?" she murmured into his neck, as their bodies swayed in time to the music, their feet barely moving.

"Well, it has been ten days and this *is* our song."

At first no one joined them on the dance floor. Laney noticed the other lounge patrons staring at them as if they were a floorshow, a few looking as if they were turned on by the sight. The old Laney would have been mortified, but this new Laney that she was morphing into found it titillating. She did a slight pelvic grind and Bryce groaned.

Couples began to join them on the floor, clinging to one another as closely as Bryce and Laney were. "I think we started something here," Bryce whispered in her ear, causing a shiver to run through her. "A lotta guys are gonna get lucky tonight, and I don't mean at the tables."

The song ended too soon. "Whoa!" the DJ said, fanning herself again. "You guys are killing me! Let's work off some of that heat with an appropriate Usher song."

The DJ Got Us Fallin' in Love began to play. Bryce led Laney off the floor and back to the stools.

"Let's get out of here," he said.

He motioned for the tab, and gave the bartender his credit card without looking at the total. He signed the ticket and threw a ten on the bar for a tip. As they turned to leave the bar, Laney saw the DJ watching them. She gave another thumbs-up and Laney grinned at her.

The cab ride back to the hotel was relaxed, Bryce with his arm around her, her head against his shoulder, her hand held in his free one. A couple of times he kissed her on her forehead. Neither of them spoke. It felt so right being with him that Laney could not fathom her reasoning for resisting it at first. Maybe he had been wiser at age four than she was at forty-one, somehow recognizing in his innocence that they were meant to be together. Life had separated them temporarily, but Fate had intervened, bringing them together again at a more appropriate time in their lives. Maybe Lady Luck did exist after all, and they had hit it big in that game of chance called life.

They took their time making love that night. The passion was there, but it was a slow burn that they teased and fanned until the flames burned long and steady. The lights in the bedroom were off, but a light from the bathroom illuminated the room enough that they could see one another clearly. They moved in unison, looking deeply into one another's eyes as they did. Bryce's eyes were full of desire for her, but more— they were full of love. Laney knew he saw the same emotions in her eyes.

Later, he fell asleep, turned on his side toward her, his arm flung across her chest, his head slightly bent and touching her shoulder. She kissed his silky hair, breathing deeply of the clean smell of it.

"I love you, Bryce Adams," she whispered, wondering why she hadn't had the courage to tell him while he was awake.

Chapter 14

They got back to town just before dark Sunday. Their day had been full, starting with breakfast at the Grille at Palm Court in the beautiful art deco Netherland Plaza, a visit to the Krohn Conservatory, and ending with a trip to the zoo. Bryce had thought they could catch a play, but nothing was scheduled for Sunday afternoon. Laney wasn't at all disappointed; she hadn't been to a zoo since Dee was in elementary school and had forgotten how much she enjoyed visiting the animals.

The couch and TV in Bryce's house were still in place, and the workers had done a great job grouting the tile and locking up after themselves. Laney had to admit Bryce's decision to install tile had been a good one; the floors looked beautiful. Because the workmen were due back early Monday morning to do the living room, they decided to stay at Laney's house, Bryce setting the alarm on his cell phone so he would be up in time to let them in.

There were two messages waiting on her home phone. The first was Greg.

"Where are you? I need to talk to you." There was a pause, then, "Damn it! Call me as soon as you get this. It's important."

Laney guessed Greg had tried the home number first, and then directed the rest of his harassing calls to her cell. She hadn't yet turned her phone back on, and she decided now it could stay off the rest of the night. It had been a perfect weekend and she wanted the rest of it to stay that way.

The other was Dee reporting in that she and her friends had stopped in Memphis and were staying with Vic's aunt and uncle.

"Oh, Mom, you wouldn't believe Beale Street! Awesome! Vic's uncle took us to watch the Peabody ducks parade through the lobby of the hotel—crazy!"

Someone said something in the background and Dee giggled.

"Jana said to tell you the guys are hot, too!"

Laney smiled at the enthusiasm in her daughter's voice. Greta was right. Dee would "deal" with the news that her mother was in love with the man she'd had her eyes on. That was one of the many good things about youth—the ability to adapt and move on. Laney suspected Bryce was already a footnote in her daughter's life, filed away as an embarrassing memory and already replaced in the present by some Tennessee hunk she had just met.

For a few seconds, Laney felt a pang of envy. By the time she was Dee's age, she was already pregnant and committed to Greg. She had missed the chance to be footloose and carefree. Still, she wouldn't change any of it. She had a beautiful, intelligent child, the marriage to Greg hadn't been all bad, and maybe it had all led her to the person she was now—a financially secure businesswoman in love with a wonderful hunk of a man.

They showered together before bed, slowly rubbing each other's body with soapy rags, rinsing off while kissing under the spray from the showerhead. As the last of the soapsuds swirled down the drain, Bryce pulled away and roughly turned her away from him, his hand pushing down on her upper back, forcing her into a bent position. Before getting into the shower, he had wisely placed a condom within reach on the back of the toilet. Laney braced herself against the wall of the shower, anticipation building as she listened to him tearing the foil wrapper. Then, he grasped her by the hips and entered her from behind, thrusting hard and deep while waves of pleasure ran through her as the water from the shower ran over her.

Afterward they dried each other with fluffy white towels, and Laney made cups of chamomile tea. They cuddled on the couch and watched Masterpiece Mystery while her hair dried. They had had more sex than sleep over the weekend, and by the time the show ended, they were both nodding off. They made it to the bed and fell asleep on their sides, Bryce's arm around her, their bodies spooned against one another.

The next morning Laney fixed pancakes while Bryce made the coffee and fried bacon, stopping from time-to-time to kiss her on the neck or pat her on the ass as he passed her in the small kitchen. Greta called while they were eating, and she and Laney arranged to meet at Starbucks mid-morning, then go for a workout at Bodies. Bryce had decided to stick around the house while the workers were there to oversee the moving of furniture. Laney wasn't sure she'd be back in time for lunch, so they agreed to meet back at her house for dinner.

After Bryce left, Laney turned her cell back on. Greg had called eleven times over the weekend—five times on Saturday, including three times after she had turned her phone off. The other six calls were spread over the day on Sunday, starting at 7AM and ending at eleven last night.

She was tempted to ignore the messages Greg had left, but she saw that Rex had called Sunday morning and again Sunday evening. It was hardly fair to ignore him, so she steeled herself for Greg's ranting and pushed the button under Listen to start the messages.

She needn't have worried. Each of Greg's messages was short and consisted of some variation of, "Where the hell are you? Are you with that son-of-a-bitch Adams? I need to talk to you—it's important." After listening to the four from Saturday Greg had left when she hadn't answered and the one he'd made early Sunday, she heard Rex's voice.

"Hey, Laney," he said. "Hoped to catch you. Just wanted to let you know I'm catching a plane in a couple of hours and will be back later today. I'll call you when I get in. Maybe we can get a late dinner."

Laney sat down hard on the stool at the table. It looked like she wasn't going to get another reprieve from dealing with Rex. A little part of her had selfishly hoped that his company's Iowa emergency would be complicated enough to keep him away longer. She would have to talk to him. The question was whether to do it over the phone or in person.

The next four messages from Greg were variations on the theme of the Saturday calls, but the fifth and final one was a little longer.

"Damn it, Laney, you need to call me! I know you're with Adams. I don't want to believe you'd team up with him against me like this just to get even for the mistakes I made, but I'm beginning to think that's exactly what you've done." His voice was getting louder, as his anger and frustration over not being able to make contact with her grew. "Well, you screwed yourself, lady. Hope that asshole was worth it. Bodies isn't for sale anymore!"

The call disconnected, and the automated menu options of what to do with the call began to play.

Bodies wasn't for sale anymore? What in heaven's name was Greg talking about, Laney wondered. Would he be spiteful enough to deprive her of the money from the sale and the chance to be free of him just to satisfy his own jealousy? It didn't make sense. Greg put his own financial self-interest above almost everything else. She just couldn't see him passing up the opportunity to make a bundle of money from the sale just to get even with her. All she could come up with was that he must have been drinking and thought saying such a thing would get her to return his call.

"It's me." Rex's message began to play. "I just got in, but I guess you're not. My flight was delayed, so I got in later than I expected. I'll try you again tomorrow, or give me a call when you can. I hope everything is okay."

Laney thought he sounded puzzled—and worried. And why wouldn't he be? Thanks to cell phones, there was seldom any reason for people to miss a call and no reason to miss a message. He was probably beginning to think something had happened to her, like an accident or something else that had put her in the hospital or the morgue. He was right that something had happened. While he was gone, she had fallen in love with his competition. She was going to have to tell him that, and she wasn't looking forward to doing so.

Later, she decided. Right now there was coffee and a workout with Greta, her go-to person for advice. Greta would know how to handle it.

***

"So whose bed were you shacked up in all weekend—yours or Bryce's?" Greta asked as soon as they sat down at the table with their Starbucks drinks and pastries. "Greg sure had his boxers in a knot. He called me a bunch of times accusing me of knowing where you were."

"Oh, Greta, I'm so sorry! I didn't know he was bothering you. I hung up on him Saturday evening, then turned my phone off."

"Don't worry about it." Greta waved her hand, dismissing Laney's apology. "Lee took care of it. After about the fifth or sixth call, Lee got on and had a man-to-man with Greg. He didn't call anymore after that."

"He called the house once and my cell eleven times. I think he's losing it. In the last message he left, he said he was withdrawing his offer to sell Bodies."

"What? Why?"

"I guess he thinks he's getting even with me for being with Bryce."

"He'll get over *that* in a hurry!" Greta snorted. "Greg's not going to pass on the bundle he'll make on that sale."

"I hope you're right."

"Of course, I'm right. Besides, you can still sell your share, can't you?"

"Legally, yes. But I doubt the buyer would go for that." Laney sighed. "If Greg sticks to his guns about this, I'll be stuck with him."

"I wouldn't worry about it." Greta patted Laney's hand. "He'll come round. Now, answer my question. Whose bed were you hiding out in?"

"Actually we hid out in a Cincinnati bed," Laney said and proceeded to tell Greta about their weekend jaunt.

"Wow!" Greta said when she finished. "Little Brycie sure knows how to romance a lady! Getting the DJ to play 'your' song by telling her it was your anniversary . . . I've never known any DJ in a club to take requests."

"Well, I'm pretty sure he gave her a big tip. He handed her something and she looked surprised when she saw it." She smiled. "It was a perfect weekend, Greta—the hotel, the dinners, the walks together, even the zoo. Not to mention the sex, of course."

"You're hooked, aren't you?"

Laney sighed. "Yeah, I am. Maybe I'm a fool, but I'm in love with a man I used to babysit—a massage therapist who takes time off whenever he wants to."

"For an unemployed massage therapist, he sure blew some bucks on you this weekend."

"Yes, he did, and that worries me. I don't like that he ran up his credit card like that."

"Maybe he thinks you're worth it."

"That's flattering, but isn't it also kind of irresponsible?" Laney said.

"You don't think . . . ?" Greta started. Then, "Nah, never mind."

"What? Finish your sentence."

"I was just going to say, could Bryce have looked at what he spent on you as an investment?"

Laney looked at Greta without speaking for a few moments, not understanding. Then, she did.

"You mean, could Greg be right? Could Bryce be after my money?"

"Well . . . the weekend does sound like it was designed to sweep you off your feet. You would be a lucrative catch for any man."

"Thanks a lot," Laney muttered.

"Hey, it's a fact. You're going to come into a pile of ready cash. While Bryce doesn't strike me as a gold-digger, you can never be sure. And," she added, "even if he is, it doesn't mean he doesn't also care for you."

Laney sat back, her coffee and bagel forgotten for the moment. Was it possible that at least a part of her attraction was the promise of her new wealth? When he kissed her and held her and made love to her, could dollar signs be part of the turn-on? She couldn't see it, but then, would she? The fact was she was naïve when it came to judging a man's motivations. She was easy pickings for someone with Bryce's looks and charm.

And maybe Greta was right. Maybe Bryce was attracted to her from the beginning, but knowing she owned a business she was selling for a large amount of money might have made her all the more desirable. Was that wrong? Didn't women often choose a man based on his financial success as well as any other attributes he might have? And didn't wealthy men often choose younger women who didn't have a dime to their name? Why did it seem so mercenary and tacky when the roles were reversed?

"You've given me a headache," she grumbled.

"Sorry, sweetie," Greta said. "I'm probably full of it. I don't really see Bryce as being like that myself, but then it's hard for me to see past those muscles and that cute smile of his anyway."

"You like that smile, too, huh?" Laney laughed.

"Oh, yeah!"

They finished their lattes and left Starbucks, still talking about the weekend. Laney shushed Greta when they got to the door of Bodies. She didn't want the employees listening to wild stories about their boss.

An hour and a half later, they had finished their workouts and their showers. As they started through the front door, they came face-to-face with Greg. Laney was shocked at his appearance. He had dark shadows under his eyes and stubble on his cheeks. She wondered if he'd slept any at all over the weekend and felt a pang of guilt for the pain she had caused him. Just as quickly as the pang of guilt manifested itself, she squashed it. She had no reason to feel guilty. She was a free woman and she could love whomever she wanted.

"Finally!" Greg said when he saw her. He looked over her shoulder, trying to see into the workout area. "Where's your boy toy? Is he here?"

"Greg, what is wrong with you?" Laney demanded. "You're making a fool of yourself!"

"I'm making a fool of *myself*? Oh, boy, that's rich!"

"Greg . . . ," Greta started.

"Greta, this isn't your concern." Greg interrupted her. He turned and opened the outer door, holding it for her. "Go on now. I need to talk to my wife."

"She's not your wife anymore, Greg," Greta said, her tone indicating she was ready to kick Greg's butt if he didn't leave Laney alone.

"It's okay, Greta." She turned to Greg. "We can talk in the office. I don't feel like making a scene on the street or in front of the employees."

Greta hesitated, reluctant to leave her. Laney nodded at her to go ahead. "I'll call you later," she said. "I promise."

With one last glare at Greg, Greta turned and left.

Greg controlled himself until the door to the office was shut. Then, he erupted.

"How *could* you do this to me, Laney? You're the mother of my child, for Christ's sake! I know you're still upset about the mistakes I made, but how could you turn on me like this?"

"Greg, I have told you it's none of your business who I date! And trust me, I'm not seeing Bryce to get even with you!"

"You expect me to believe that?"

"I don't care what you believe! We are through, and we have been through for three years. You need to accept that."

Greg began pacing back and forth across the office, running his fingers through his hair, leaving it standing in spikes. Laney watched him, starting to feel a little scared. She had never seen him like this. Had he been drinking? She hadn't noticed the smell of alcohol on him, but maybe he'd had something fairly odorless like vodka.

"He's not getting Bodies. Maybe I can't keep him from stealing my wife, but I can keep him from getting Bodies."

"Greg, you are making absolutely *no* sense! If we've already sold Bodies, how could Bryce get it? No matter how serious he and I might become, Bodies would already belong to someone else."

"Yeah, *him*!" Greg stopped pacing and glared at her, his fists clenched. "I won't let that happen."

"What are you talking about?" Greg not only looked like a crazy man, he sounded like one.

Greg glared at her for several seconds before his fists finally unclenched. "You really don't know, do you?" he said.

"Know what?"

"My private investigator got back to me late Friday. Bryce Adams is our buyer."

"What? That's impossible! Your investigator must be mistaken."

"Apparently his father came from money. He and a couple of cousins took their inheritance from their grandparents and parlayed it into a chain of health clubs and other investments. He doesn't look like it, but the son-of-a-bitch has the reputation of being a genius when it comes to business."

Laney stared at him, her mouth hanging open, trying to process the words she had just heard. Bryce, the unemployed massage therapist, was the buyer for Bodies? Bryce, the man she had worried was spending too much money on her in Cincinnati, had enough money to buy Bodies? The man whose wardrobe seemed to consist mainly of jeans and tees was a financial genius?

She chuckled, then began to laugh, and suddenly she was bent over, roaring with laughter, tears running down her face. Greg looked dumbfounded by her mirth, the expression on his face that of a bullied little boy. It should have made her feel bad for him, but instead it stoked her laughter. She collapsed into her desk chair, fighting for breath and wiping at her face. Her stomach hurt and she couldn't breath, but she was unable to stop.

"You find this funny?" Greg said, the hurt little boy trying to sound indignant. "You enjoy laughing at me?"

"I'm not laughing at you." Laney managed to get out between gasps for breaths as she struggled to control her laughter.

"What's so funny then?" Greg demanded. "If you really didn't know Adams is our buyer, then he's been stringing you along, too. That should make you angry. But instead, you seem to think it's funny."

"What I think is funny . . . ," Laney started, stopped to let a chuckle escape, and moaned. "Oh, Lord, this is killing me!"

She opened a desk drawer, pulled out a handful of tissues, and dabbed at her eyes, still chortling.

"Oh! Whew!" She took a deep breath and shuddered. Her stomach felt like she had just done a hundred sit-ups. She tried again. "What I think is funny is that *you* thought he was after my money!"

She went off into gales of laughter again, bent over in her chair. Greg would probably lose it any time now and murder her in a fit of domestic rage, but there was nothing she could do to stop the laughter. Maybe she should be upset with Bryce for not telling her, but she would decide that later. For now, the entire thing was too funny to be upset over.

Greg didn't lose it. Instead, he sat down in the chair in front of her desk, put his head in his hands and waited while her laughter ran its course. Finally she straightened, blew her nose and wiped her eyes.

"Oh, wow! Sorry about that," she said. "I just couldn't help it."

Greg sat up, but didn't respond.

"Are you sure about Bryce being our buyer?" Laney said.

Greg nodded. "I'm sure. He and his cousins are co-owners of the holding company that made the offer. They own over sixty clubs in fourteen states. Plus a bunch of other properties."

"My God!" Laney said. "He doesn't look or act like a tycoon, but he *is* one? I would never have guessed."

"And you're not upset about that? That he didn't tell you, I mean?"

"He must have had his reasons."

"You can bet they were underhanded ones!"

"Why? What could he possibly have gained from keeping me in the dark?" Laney said. "It's not like he had his attorneys make us a lowball offer before or after he started pursuing me. I can't see how it benefitted him to be undercover, so to speak."

"Then why didn't he tell you?" Greg demanded.

Why, indeed, Laney wondered, but thought she had an idea why. Hadn't she realized a few days ago that now that she was going to have a lot of money, she would always have to worry if men were interested in her for herself or for what she had? It sounded like Bryce had a lot more than she would have after the Bodies sale. Maybe he wanted her to fall in love with him for himself without the added complication of knowing he was wealthy. It had worked. She had fallen in love with a massage therapist.

"Greg," she said. "You don't want to keep Bodies, do you? Not really. Not just to spite Bryce."

"We can find another buyer." He jutted his chin out. "Adams isn't the only game in town."

"How do you think another buyer is going to look at you backing out of a sale just as it was about to be finalized?" she said. "Would you make an offer to someone that unpredictable?"

"Then, we'll keep it," Greg said. "We made a good living from Bodies. We'll keep it and pass it on to Dee one day."

"Dee has her own way to make in life," Laney said. "And there's no 'we' in this, Greg. I'm not keeping the clubs. I can sell my half to Bryce, and you can be partners with him."

Greg looked stricken. "You wouldn't!"

"I would."

"He . . . why would he go for that?"

"He'll go for it, because he's in love with me." As soon as she said it, Laney knew it was true. "It's the same reason he didn't tell me he was our buyer. He wanted me to fall in love with him without money getting in the way, and he'll complete the sale for the same reason. He'll want me to be financially independent so money doesn't influence any decision I make about us."

"Are you? Falling in love with him, I mean."

Laney looked at Greg for a few moments without speaking. She had loved him once. Most of their years together had been good ones, and they could have spent a lifetime together. She felt a pang of sadness realizing that their chance for that was gone, never to be recovered.

"I already have," she said.

He looked back at her, no longer angry, but resigned. Finally he nodded.

"Okay," he said. "I won't stop the sale. Maybe the son-of-a-bitch isn't all bad, but I don't want to be partners with him."

He smiled, a hint of the old Greg in his expression, and she smiled back.

"Thank you," she said.

Greg stood and came around to her side of the desk. He took her hand and pulled her to her feet, only a few inches between them. "You tell Adams he'd better treat you right," he murmured. "Tell him to learn from my mistakes."

He looked at her for a few seconds more as if he were trying to memorize what she looked like, then kissed her on the forehead. Releasing her, he turned and walked to the door.

"Wait." She crossed the room to him, reached up and gently smoothed his hair down.

"Your hair was sticking up," she said.

"Thanks." He smiled, but his eyes were sad. "Be happy, Laney. You deserve it."

He turned and was gone—not just from the room, but finally, she knew, from her life.

***

She remained in the office for a while after Greg left. At first, she sat and replayed their conversation, then her thoughts drifted back to their years together. She felt like she was having a solo memorial service for their marriage, something she had been unable to do in the aftermath of his infidelity and the divorce. Thanks to Bryce, the rawness of that betrayal had healed. She was in love and ready to be loved in return. She was finally able to forgive Greg and move on.

Eventually she stood, collected her purse and went downstairs. She was lost in thought as she exited the club and didn't see Rex until he spoke her name.

"Oh," she said, surprised, feeling herself start to flush. First Greg, now Rex. Maybe she should have used the club's back door. "Hello."

"Hey," he said. "Thought I'd get in a workout and hoped I'd catch you here. I've left you a couple of messages?"

He stopped, waiting for an explanation. Might as well get this over with, Laney thought.

"I had my phone turned off over the weekend," she said. "Problems with Greg."

"Oh?" Rex straightened.

"It's all worked out now." She waved a hand dismissively, her eyes looking everywhere but at him. "I did hear your messages when I turned it back on, and I apologize for not calling you back."

He waited. She took a deep breath and forced herself to look into those gorgeous blue eyes.

"I don't think I can see you anymore, Rex. I'm sorry."

He looked at her for a moment, then that slow sexy smile started moving across his face. "Let me guess. Adams got back to town before I did, right?"

Laney could feel herself blushing. She nodded. "I'm sorry."

"Hey, don't apologize. He seems like a nice guy. Not as nice as me, of course. . . ."

He laughed, she laughed, and just like that her nervousness was gone. She looked at him standing there, smiling that incredibly sexy smile, his blue eyes twinkling. She couldn't stop herself from remembering how it had felt to be pressed against his body when they danced and kissed by the back booth at the Moonglow. His expression changed slightly, and she realized her thoughts must have been showing on her face. She looked away quickly.

Greta was right. Too many men, too little time!

"Well, I guess I'd better be going," she said. "I suppose you'll be going back to Atlanta soon?"

He nodded, still with that smile on his face. Damn him!

"Nothing to stick around here for," he said. "Unless you think Adams might be taking another trip soon."

"Rex . . . ," she started, but he laughed.

"Only kidding, Laney. Well, not entirely, but I doubt you're the kind of woman who would go for a deal like that. Unfortunately for me."

He stepped closer, placed the tips of the fingers of his right hand under her chin and tilted it toward him. She didn't move as his lips touched hers and lingered there for several seconds.

"If Adams ever screws up and loses you," he whispered, "Joanna and Bill know how to get in touch with me."

She didn't know how to reply to that, so she simply nodded.

"Bye, Laney." He turned and entered the club. Patti was just exiting on her way to lunch. Her eyes followed Rex as he stepped through the inner door of the club, then she turned back to Laney.

"Whew! We are gonna miss you around here, boss lady," she said. "Thanks to all the hunky men following you around, it's been an interesting place to work! And just when things are getting good, you go and leave us!"

Laney laughed. "Ah, Patti, if you only knew!"

***

Bryce came out of his house when he saw her car pull into the drive. As she got out of the driver's side, he pulled her to him and gave her a lingering kiss. She returned it, no longer concerned with what the neighbors might see.

"Glad you made it back in time for lunch," he murmured. "Maybe we should make a couple of sandwiches and eat them in bed."

She laughed and shook her head. "Uh-uh. Too many crumbs."

"You get any on you, I'll lick them off."

"Maybe some other time." She pushed him away. "For now, we're going to eat in the kitchen and have a serious talk."

"Uh-oh. Should I be worried?"

"I don't know. Should you?"

She stepped around him and started for her house, enjoying the concern that was starting to show on his face. Suddenly she noticed something and stopped. The For Sale sign was gone from the front yard of Bryce's grandmother's house. She felt her heart drop. Had it sold already? Did that mean he would be leaving for California sooner than she had thought? The Bodies closing was this Friday. Maybe there would be nothing to keep him in town after all his business was concluded.

"What happened to the sign?" She turned to him. "Has the house sold already?"

"Sure did." He nodded, but didn't offer any further details.

"Oh." She started walking toward her front door, her insecurity rising to the surface. What had she been thinking? That the house would never sell, and he would simply be the sexy "boy next door" forever? Why did life have to be so complicated?

In the house, Bryce headed straight for the refrigerator and began lining sandwich fixings up on the counter. She dropped her workout clothes in the washer located in the closet in the hall just off the kitchen, watching him while he took plates out of the cabinet and put bread in the toaster. He seemed at home in her kitchen. It seemed so right that he was there, just as it seemed so right he was in her life. When she tried to imagine him gone from it, she felt a pain in her chest, and for a few seconds, she wished she had never let him get close.

"Do you want chicken salad or a ham sandwich?" he asked.

"Chicken salad, I think," she said. "But I can fix them."

"I got it. What do you want to drink?"

"I'll make coffee."

"Sounds good. I can use some more caffeine. I'm still recovering from the weekend."

He quickly made her chicken salad sandwich, choosing ham for himself. She started the coffee and pulled a bag of chips from the pantry. When he set the sandwich plates on the table, she halted the coffee long enough to pour two cups, and sat down across from him.

"The house sold fast," she said. "I didn't know there had even been a showing."

"There hasn't been," he said.

"And it still sold?" she said, surprised. "How did that happen?"

"I bought it." He took a huge bite of his ham sandwich and chewed while he watched her reaction, that adorable crooked grin on his face.

Laney stared at him for a moment, the sandwich she held in her hands forgotten. Then, she started to smile, feeling her spirits lift again. He'd bought the house! That had to mean he wasn't planning on going anywhere, didn't it?

"You?" She laid the sandwich back on her plate and sat back. "Guess you're buying up a lot of things around town, aren't you?"

He stopped smiling. Laney was gratified to see a slight blush on his face.

"Uh . . . ," he started, probably intending to act like he didn't know what she was talking about. After a few seconds, he gave up the attempt. "I guess Greg's PI is good at what he does, huh?"

"He is," she said. "Why didn't you tell me you were our buyer? You had to know I'd find out eventually."

He sighed. "When we made the offer, Laney, I didn't know you were one of the owners. I swear. I remember noticing your first name and remembering the babysitter I was so crazy about, but the last name was different. I didn't think anymore about it. When you came to the door that first night and I learned your last name was Mitchell, I was surprised. We—my partners and I—always make our offers through the company and try to keep our names out of it until things are settled. So I kept my mouth shut."

He reached across the table and took her hand.

"I wanted you the minute I laid eyes on you that first night, and when I didn't say anything right away, it got harder and harder to tell you. Besides, I didn't want the fact I was your buyer interfering with what we might have between us."

"Afraid I might be after your money?" she said, smiling.

He shook his head. "More afraid that the money might screw it up."

"So what were you going to do? Let me walk into the closing next Friday and find out then?"

"No, no, of course not!" He shook his head. "I wasn't even planning on coming to the closing. The attorneys can sign on behalf of my partners and me."

"Oh, that's just great!" Laney was starting to get angry. She yanked her hand out of his. "So you weren't going to tell me at all?"

"Of course I was going to tell you." Bryce took her hand again. When she tried to pull away, he tightened his grip. "Laney, please. I was going to tell you before the closing, but I wasn't going to attend because of Greg. I didn't think he'd find out before then, and I knew he'd probably throw a fit if I showed up at the closing."

"Well, you're right about that. He would probably have refused to sell. That was his first reaction when he got the report from the detective he hired. You don't have to worry about that now," she added. "I told him

I'd sell you my half and he could be partners with you. That convinced him that he should still go through with the sale."

"I'm sorry, Laney." His eyes were serious as he looked at her—and something more. He looked scared. "I didn't intend to cause you problems. I swear I was going to tell you before the closing. I wanted to tell you while we were in Cincinnati, but everything was so perfect, I didn't want to ruin it."

"Secrets are what ruin things, Bryce, not the truth."

"You're right. But money has a way of doing that, too. I wanted to make an impression on you before you knew who I was."

He grinned that cute little grin again.

"And unless I'm very much mistaken, I've managed to do that." He stood, came around to her side of the table, put his hands on her waist and lifted her to a standing position. "Haven't I?"

She scowled at him, but felt the scowl morphing into a smile. It was impossible to stay angry with him—especially when he was standing so close.

"Well, you can relax," she said. "I'm not after your money. Just your body."

"Not that I'm complaining, but is that all you want? I know I want more than that. I love you, Laney. It may sound silly, but I'm not kidding when I say I think I fell in love with you when I was four and you were fifteen. The minute I saw you at my front door, I knew that."

She started to speak, but he shushed her.

"I'm not asking you for a commitment now. There's no rush. I bought Grandma's house so I'd have a place to woo you from."

"Woo me?" Laney began to laugh.

"Yeah, I'm old-fashioned that way," he said, still grinning. "I'll have to leave occasionally to take care of business, but I plan on spending every minute I can with you. We can head out to California, we can travel to Europe or Asia or Antarctica if that's what you want—or we can stay right here. And if you don't want to ever move away, that's fine with me, too. I like this town and I like this neighborhood. The best thing about what I do for a living is that I don't have to answer to a boss and I can do my job from just about anywhere."

He pulled her close to him and kissed her lightly on the lips.

"So what do you say? You going to give me a chance to make you love me?"

Her arms slid around his broad strong back.

"You haven't changed a bit, you know that?" she said. "When you were little, you never gave up on something you wanted whether it was another story or a treat. You were always so determined to get your way."

"Is that a problem?"

"Not at all." She smiled. "Determination is a trait I prefer in the man I love."

His eyes widened in surprise and pleasure. She twisted his silky hair around her fingers and pulled his face to hers. As their lips touched, she decided it had been a good idea to take that babysitting job after all.

###

About the Author

Lolli Powell writes contemporary romance, romantic suspense, and cozy mystery novels. She lives with her husband, four dogs, and two cats inside Daniel Boone National Forest in Kentucky.

You can contact Lolli Powell at:
Website: http://www.lollipowell.com
Blog: http://www.ridgewriter.com
Facebook: https://www.facebook.com/lollipowell/